GHOST'S DILEMMA

Witch's Apprentice, Book Two

Morwen Navarre

A NineStar Press Publication

Published by NineStar Press
P.O. Box 91792,
Albuquerque, New Mexico, 87199 USA.
www.ninestarpress.com

Ghost's Dilemma

Printed in the USA
First Edition
July, 2018

Print ISBN: 978-1-949340-39-6

Also available in eBook, ISBN: 978-1-949340-31-0

Warning: This book contains sexually explicit content, which may only be suitable for mature readers.

Ghost is content to spend all his free time with Gerry. But scandal and hate surrounding Ghost's appointment as the first male witch, along with a deadly epidemic, force Ghost to make choices that will separate him from his love.

Spurred on by a message from his mentor, Ghost embarks on a journey through mystical underground tunnels and lost civilizations to the frozen lands of his origin, seeking a way to neutralize the threat back home. While he struggles to find a balance between his duties as a witch and his calling as a seer, all Ghost really wants is to return to the haven he has found in Gerry's arms.

To my Neko who lifts me up;

To Pip who gives me courage;

To my readers who make it all worthwhile.

Prologue

GERRY STRODE DOWN the slate path beside the house, toward the familiar and rhythmic sound of Ghost chopping herbs. Ghost was absorbed in his work at his bench, so Gerry took the opportunity to stand in the doorway and admire Ghost from behind. His snowy white hair was tied in a messy tail hanging between his shoulder blades. His pert buttocks presented an enticing sight in his smooth leather breeches. Although he stood just a bit over sixteen hands in height, his lean muscles rippled under his shirt as he trimmed and tied the herbs to be dried. While Ghost finished hanging a bundle of greens by the stem, Gerry snuck up and wrapped his arms around Ghost's middle. Ghost startled, then laughed and relaxed against Gerry.

Do I smell scones?" Gerry asked into Ghost's ear. Ghost turned to face him, and Gerry stole a playful kiss. His hip brushed against the curve of Ghost's rear.

Ghost leaned back into the embrace. "I had the time this morning. The sole visitor I had was a woman with a deep cut. She slipped when she was chopping root vegetables and the knife went clean to the bone." Ghost wriggled free from Gerry's embrace. "Now, let me wash up and we'll eat."

Gerry patted Ghost's rear as Ghost walked past him. Ghost ducked his head and smiled. Gerry followed him into the yard, enjoying the view as Ghost rinsed from the bucket by the well.

"I saw the godsman today." Ghost stiffened enough for it to be perceptible before Gerry continued. "He says we can make it official at the full moon."

Six moons had passed since the godsman had refused to perform the rite for them, claiming Gerry and Ghost had not had a proper courtship and could not be sure of their convictions in such a short time.

"If you still want to, of course. And if you can last another quarter moon."

Ghost spun and launched himself into Gerry's arms. Gerry laughed as Ghost buried his wet hands in Gerry's hair and pulled Gerry down into a heated kiss.

When Ghost finally let Gerry up, Gerry gazed into Ghost's ice-blue eyes and smiled. "I'll take the kiss for a yes." Ghost opened his mouth to speak, but Gerry touched his finger to Ghost's lips to stop him. "And I'm also going to tell you I'm the happiest man in the village right now. I love you, Ghost. I'd lay down my life to protect you, and I won't ever let you be harmed. You'll always be safe right here in my arms if you accept my offer to be my mate and bind yourself to me."

"Of course the kiss is a yes." Ghost's eyes glistened like ice melting in the sun, and his lips trembled through his smile. "I'll bind myself to you gladly, Gerry. I trust you to keep me safe, even when I'm reckless, and I know you'll protect me from whatever goes wrong. Your arms are my sanctuary when I'm ready to give up because I know you'll be strong for me. And I love you. I'll love you for as long as I live."

THE FULL MOON finally arrived, and Ghost and Gerry dressed in their best clothing to appear in the gods' house.

Gerry brushed Ghost's hair until his long tresses shone. Ghost's nimble fingers danced along the line of bone buttons on Gerry's shirt. The traditional gift to the gods, consisting of a fat runner and a cask of mead, had been accepted and left on the offering table.

Gerry listened to the godsman's droning voice. Ghost stood beside him. Both of them faced the gods' wall, decorated with carved masks for the Seven and a blank mask for the Eighth.

"As our gods themselves have done, you come to take an oath to bind yourselves together. Ghost, you will no longer be solely Gerry's dependent. You will be Gerry's mate, first in Gerry's heart. Gerry, you will no longer be solely Ghost's alpha. You will be Ghost's mate, first in Ghost's heart. You must give each other unconditional love and trust, setting the needs of the other above your own. Gerry, you must protect Ghost and guide him. Ghost, you must trust Gerry's judgment and let him guide you. Above all, you must not forsake the oath you take today in the sight of the gods."

The godsman placed Ghost's hand in Gerry's. As he wrapped a thin red cord around their wrists, he said, "The Father and the Lady. He protects and she guides. The Hunter and the Farmer. He culls and she nurtures. The Sea and the Moon. He sends dreams and she awakens love. The Seeker and he whose name shall remain unspoken. Let all the gods bear witness to your oath."

Gerry turned to gaze into Ghost's clear blue eyes, seeing joy and love reflected back. "I offer you my protection and my love. I will care for you and keep you from harm for all of my days. You will be first in my heart, Ghost. Before the gods, this is my oath to you."

Ghost's voice was strong. "I accept your protection and your love, and offer you my love for all of my days. I will trust in your care and find safety at your side. I will care for you, and you will be first in my heart, Gerry. Before the gods, this is my oath to you."

The godsman tied a loose knot in the cord that joined their wrists. "May the gods smile upon you both and bless this mating."

The cord around their wrists did nothing to dampen the ardor of the kiss Gerry bestowed on Ghost, a kiss Ghost returned with equal enthusiasm. They were mated now, and Gerry's elation could not be contained as he claimed his beloved witch for his own.

Chapter One

ALMOST TWO MOONS had passed since Ghost and Gerry had taken their vows. Midsummer was approaching, and Gerry had decided to take advantage of the good weather to hunt with Mother, Gerry's former alpha. Mother kept his word and allowed Gerry to continue to work with him as hunter and guard. Gerry had left for the hunt before the sun rose that morning.

Ghost had grown more popular with the villagers. The Witch had taken to sending people to Ghost rather than treating them herself. Ghost frowned at her, but he saw to the patients she referred, and his remedies were effective. The word spread quickly, helped in part because he did not demand a drop of blood from them as the Witch did for her Seeker's box. Ghost simply examined the wound or sore limb and then set about remedying the complaint. He took what was offered in trade with gratitude, and if a patient had nothing to offer, he healed them anyway.

Ghost glanced up from his formulary, a journal of remedies and lore painstakingly copied by hand, his head aching after spending the morning squinting at the faded printing. He listened to the sound of the wind in the trees, and he smelled the heat of summer beneath the crisp morning air. He stood, stretched until his back creaked, and went into the back room he kept for villagers in need of monitoring.

The woman in the bed, her face pale and damp with sweat, did not seem to notice when Ghost walked into the room. He could not recall her name, but he knew the woman's alpha, Moran, in passing, having patched the surly man up once or twice after an altercation at the mead house. Moran was one of the carpenters of the village. The family should have been comfortable enough with the goods and services their alpha earned in trade, but the lure of the mead house proved stronger to Moran than his duties to his partner and dependents.

Ghost had seen the marks on the woman's upper arms. She had claimed the waters broke right before she came to Ghost, but the moment he had touched the woman's belly, he had known exactly what had transpired. As a seer, he did not need a Seeker's box to tell him. He *saw* the history of her bruises and the moment when her sac had ruptured.

Moran had been drunk, and he had come home late enough to ensure dinner was spoiled. Instead of admitting the fault lay with him, Moran lashed out, and when the woman fell, her water broke. This had been two days earlier, and had she come right away, Ghost might have given her an herbal infusion to bring on the birthing. But now, Ghost was not certain if the woman or her babe would survive. The child within her womb was close to being born, yet this fever wracking the woman troubled Ghost.

Ghost rested one hand on her rounded stomach, the peridot spiral on his forehead growing warmer as he pushed to *see*. He wondered if Moran realized his stroke of luck in having Ghost as the village's witch. The Witch would have been far harsher in her response to those marks. But she was gone now, with no word as to when, if ever, she would return.

Ghost walked a finer line, though. He was the only male witch in far too many generations to be tallied, and the sisterhood was still divided over his status. A small but vocal number of the witchsisters thought Ghost was an abomination. Although the Witch's voice had carried sufficient weight to ensure none of the dissenters would lash out at him for now, Ghost was aware it would take no more than a small error, and he would find himself hunted without mercy.

At the moment, Ghost had no time to waste thinking about what could happen. He needed to act, or he would lose the woman and her babe. It might take the Seeker's mercy as well as all of Ghost's skill to save them both. The Witch had given him some rare herbs before she left, which were at the ready if Ghost had need for them. Ghost had prepared a serum of willow bark and plantain for the Seeker's kiss, a tubular relic of gleaming metal used to administer the various extracts he prepared. The Seeker's kiss stung at first, but the subsequent relief was well worth the momentary discomfort.

Ghost inserted the serum into a glass cylinder and placed it in the body of the Seeker's kiss. As he closed the rounded end, the relic emitted a glowing light, indicating it was ready to use. Ghost murmured a small prayer to the Seeker herself before he applied it to the woman's arm. He pressed the lighted dome and heard the familiar hiss as it worked, but the woman barely twitched. Her belly contracted, and Ghost laid his hand on it again to feel and *see* within.

The babe was ready. Doubt or indecision now would only get in the way of what needed to be done. Ghost took a deep breath to focus. Hot water waited by the hearth. He had more than enough clean linens and birthing blankets prepared. He had also ensured the witchglass on the roof had fed his gods' light with sufficient energy gathered from sunlight. The gods' light could cauterize any bleeding, should he encounter a problem.

"All right, little dam," Ghost said in as soothing a tone as he could manage. "Your babe wants to come out into the world, so let's get him born."

Delivering a baby would be harder with the woman lying supine, but she was too feverish and weak to risk letting her sit on a birthing stool. Ghost had no apprentice to help him, and he dared not take a chance of her enduring another fall. It would be a challenge, but it could be done. He used rolled blankets to lift the woman's head and shoulders as much as possible, and he coaxed her legs into bending, her feet flat on the bed.

Ghost checked and observed the crown of the head, dark and vivid as it pressed against reluctant flesh. There was no visible putrefaction, and he breathed a small prayer of thanks. If the gods were kind, this might yet end well. Ghost took another fortifying breath and went to work.

GERRY HEFTED THE massive runner onto the hook in the meat house. Conn had tracked a fine herd of the long-legged herbivores for them, taking one down on his own with a well-placed arrow. Gerry had kept the fat buck and traded the rest of his share of the runners for a generous sum of tally sticks. To celebrate, Gerry intended to take Ghost to the market to select a few treats from the shipment of exotic goods that had arrived from the South.

A thin wail from the house interrupted Gerry's thoughts. He sprinted up the path and into the house. "Ghost?" he called out, dashing through the kitchen and past the hearth fire.

"I'm here." Ghost came out of the back bedroom, the one Gerry thought of as the sick room. "I was tending Moran's dependent. She birthed today."

Gerry saw the tension in Ghost's face. "Not good?"

Ghost lifted one shoulder in a shrug. "She's young to be a dam, and her waters broke sooner than she claims. The babe seems strong, and I think her fever's coming down."

"Wait, this isn't his partner?" Gerry held out his arms to Ghost. "Don't tell me this is the girl he took in last Harvesttide."

Ghost walked into Gerry's embrace and rested his head on Gerry's shoulder. "The very one. Moran drinks too much mead, and then he behaves like an ass. Or in this case, a stiff cock without any regard for her welfare."

Gerry bit back a choice curse, clearing his throat a little instead. "It's not how an alpha is supposed to behave."

"He hit her." Ghost's voice was muffled by Gerry's shoulder. "He grabbed her by her upper arms, and he hit her because he was late and the dinner was spoiled. He was rough, and her water broke, but he wouldn't let her come to me right away. I *saw* it."

Gerry tightened his hold on Ghost. Ghost spoke again, voice still muffled. "His partner pretends not to notice. I can't understand it. Well, I can understand her not minding Moran taking to the girl's bed, but the rough treatment? Moran is lucky the Witch is gone. She wouldn't be debating what to do."

"I don't think I want to know, do I?" Gerry said, stroking Ghost's back to soothe him.

"Let's just say there's a reason witches are feared as well as revered." Ghost looked up and gave Gerry a tentative smile. "Go wash up. I've got some fresh-laid eggs for you, and sausages too. I'll start those cooking."

Gerry hummed into Ghost's silky, white hair. "I hung a runner in the meat house. I'll gut and dress it after we eat. And I'll bring you the liver when I'm done washing."

GHOST AND GERRY ate together in companionable silence. Ghost had set the liver to simmer by the hearth fire, intending to make a paste of it to be mixed with rendered fat, hard-cooked eggs, sweet onion, spices, and herbs. He would shape the mix into a loaf and seal it with a thick layer of meat jelly. Sliced and served on bread, it was a tasty meal.

As Gerry went out to dress the runner, Ghost heard the woman wake and went to check on her. She was pale, and her cheeks were flushed with fever, but her forehead felt cooler under Ghost's hand. He smiled at her. "You're awake. Do you remember where you are?"

"You're the witch," the woman said. "Did Moran bring me?"

Ghost managed to bite back the words he wanted to say. "You came alone, little dam. You were feverish, and your babe wanted to be born."

The woman struggled to sit up, and Ghost reached out to help her, his arm around her frail shoulders. "The baby," she whispered, and her eyes welled with tears.

"He's fine." Ghost pointed to the small cradle by the bed where the babe slept peacefully. "A strong boy, who'll be hungry when he wakes. This means we need to feed you, little dam."

"Can I hold him?" The woman dared to peer up at Ghost, and he could see the shadow of the pretty child she had been not so long before.

"I don't see why not," Ghost said. He lifted the swaddled infant and placed him in the woman's arms, watching her face light up as she touched a downy cheek. "I'm going to get some broth and bread for you, and fennel to help your milk come in strong."

Ghost went into the kitchen and ladled out a bowl of broth from the small kettle he had set to heat earlier. He cut a few thick slices of bread and went over to his workbench to make up the infusion for the young woman. He added a pinch of willow bark for the last of the fever, and plenty of honey to make it sweet.

The woman looked up when Ghost returned, and her smile was stronger. "He's so beautiful," she whispered.

Ghost set the tray on the small table beside the bed. "He is." Ghost held out his arms for the infant. "I'll hold him while you eat. Make sure you finish everything. He looks like he'll have a good appetite, and you need to eat enough to feed you both until he's weaned."

The woman dipped some bread in the broth, and to Ghost's eyes, she was forcing herself to eat slowly.

"I wasn't very hungry, with the babe coming," the woman said, reaching for a second slice. She looked down, tearing off a piece to wet in the broth.

"I don't imagine you were," Ghost said, and he did his best to be gentle. "But now you'll try to eat, for his sake. You need to be strong for him. If you need me to speak to your alpha, I can do so."

"No!" The young woman looked up, and Ghost wondered if it was fear he saw in her eyes. "Please don't, good witch, you don't need to." She swallowed hard and looked down again. "I'll make sure I eat enough. I promise. Moran will be happy I have a boy."

Ghost managed a smile for the woman, but heat bloomed in the peridot spiral on his forehead. He was not entirely sure being in Moran's favor was the best thing for this woman, but her choice of alpha was not a matter he could control. Gerry could bring a case before the elders if action was needed.

Ghost heard footsteps in the house and called out, "I'm in here!" Gerry appeared in the doorway, strong and solid, and Ghost smiled at his alpha and mate, his heart lifting at the sight of Gerry.

Gerry's dark-brown hair was longer now, like a proper alpha's hair, and his mud-green eyes lit up when he saw Ghost. "I'm rendering the fat now. Did you need me for anything while you're tending to your healing?" Gerry looked at the young girl. "Lady smile on you, little dam. I'm Gerry. What are you called?"

The woman looked nervous, her fingers plucking at the sheet covering her. "I'm Sari, good alpha, and thank you for asking."

"Gerry is fine. You're welcome in this house," Gerry said. He looked back over at Ghost, waiting for his answer.

"I could use more jelly, so some good stock bones would be nice, love." Ghost could see confusion in the woman's eyes. "Oh, and stir the big pot on your way back out?"

Gerry assented. "I'll see you in a little while, then, once I've got the meat all sorted."

Ghost waited until Gerry was gone. He was still unsure about many aspects of dealing with people, and so he resorted to being fairly direct. He knew being a witch did allow for certain eccentricities.

"Gerry is my alpha, and my vowed mate. We don't stand on a lot of ceremony between us." Ghost shrugged one shoulder. "Most witches are alphas in their own right, so maybe he respects my opinions. Gerry's alpha, the one who raised him, wasn't much for ceremony either. You aren't an alpha solely because you like to make rules. There's more, like caring about what happens to your dependents." Ghost gestured at the rest of the broth and bread. "For now, eat up, and then let's see if this little one wants to eat. But you'll stay here until you're strong enough to care for him, on my word as a witch. Your alpha can say what he will, but I'll not budge."

The babe woke and nursed, Sari marveling at her son the entire while. Ghost waited until the babe was asleep again before examining the woman, relieved to see no signs of infection. She was cool to the touch, her fever abating well. Ghost tucked her in to let her rest and offered a silent prayer of thanks to the Seeker.

THE REST OF the afternoon passed in the usual fashion. Gerry hummed as he sat by the hearth in the main room, carving needles from the long bones of a runner. The late day sun warmed the room, and a delicious smell of herbs permeated the house from Ghost's sausages. As was custom, their olive-green door stood partially open to let anyone passing know they were at home and welcomed visitors. In the sick room, Sari and her baby slept in peace.

Gerry barely looked up as a shadow filled the doorway. "Lady smile on you," Gerry said, the greeting automatic. He paused in his carving as Ghost walked in from the kitchen, stopping at the edge of the main room.

"You've got my dependent here." Moran folded his arms over his chest, a glower on his face. The smell of mead surrounded him.

Ghost did not give Gerry a chance to speak. He crossed the room and blocked Moran with a small frown, the peridot spiral on his forehead catching the sun in a sudden flare of green. "Sari birthed this morning. She had a fever when she arrived, and she was hardly able to stand. She needs watching."

"I was speaking to your alpha," Moran said and turned his back on Ghost.

Gerry watched Ghost reach out and grab Moran's arm to get the man's attention. Gerry set his carving aside, prepared to defend Ghost if need be.

"You'll speak with me. I'm this village's witch, and matters of healing are mine to decide." Ghost's frown deepened. "Her fever didn't start today. How long was she ill?"

"She was fine, and I'll have her back now." Moran moved a step closer to Ghost, and Gerry stood. A strange, cold calm swept through Gerry. He had felt the same inner chill when he had killed a rogue ranger in the ruins of an ancient city to protect Ghost and Conn, Mother's dependent.

"You're not fit to have her back." Ghost did not move. He glared up at Moran without wavering, and Gerry felt a surge of pride underneath his apprehension. "I *saw* the bruises on her. Will you invite a witch's judgment, or will you abide by my decision as a healer?"

"Don't threaten me, you Norther whelp," Moran growled.

Gerry hitched a breath as Ghost's spiral brightened, and Moran fell back a step.

"I'm a witch as well as a Norther whelp, and you'd do well to remember it, Moran," Ghost said. "Sari stays until her fever is gone and she can care for the babe. When she returns to your house, she'll need proper meals and rest for her sake and her son's. Will you hear my fee?"

"She has a son?" Moran's voice changed timbre. "Can I see her? And him? Can I see our boy?"

Ghost looked thoughtful for a moment. He relented after a long pause and led Moran to the sick room as Gerry followed close behind them. Moran peered in at the sleeping woman and her baby. When Moran turned away from the sick room, the man's cheeks were wet with tears.

"Name your fee, healer." Moran wiped at his cheeks with the backs of his hands.

Ghost picked up a small pottery jar. "A cabinet with compartments for jars this size, and drawers below for bandage linen and whatever else I might need to store."

"Done. I'll start in the morning." Moran hesitated. "A son." He shook his head and rubbed his face with his hand. He turned and looked straight into Ghost's eyes. "I'll do better for them, healer."

"You can start by staying out of the mead house," Ghost retorted. "Come by tomorrow to see her. I'll know more about when she can go home."

Gerry watched Moran leave. He walked up behind Ghost and embraced Ghost's smaller frame. "I thought I was going to have to throw him out," Gerry admitted. He buried his face in the fragrant silk of Ghost's hair. "If he'd laid a hand on you, I'd have been hard-pressed not to beat him fucking senseless."

"He's a bully," Ghost said, leaning back into Gerry. "They don't know how to react when you're not afraid of them. Let's see if he can keep his word about the mead house, though. If he doesn't, he'll have to deal with me again, and I won't be so nice."

Gerry chuckled. "You're getting fierce. I was waiting for you to curse him on the spot. Some terrible witch's curse. His eyeballs rolling back or some other dire thing."

Ghost turned, and his forehead wrinkled in a frown. "We don't actually do those things," he said as he backed out of Gerry's hold. "Witches don't cast spells or curse people. Maybe in the stories sung in the mead house, but not in real life. We use the old lore to heal people. We read the ancient language so we can learn how to use the relics the rangers scavenge. Like my Seeker's kiss, or the gods' light. The relics are tools the ancient healers used."

Ghost gave Gerry a mischievous grin, his expression lightening again. "The Witch told me stories of places she called 'libraries,' filled with books. People could come and borrow books to read, and they'd return those books so they could borrow still more books. I fell in love with the notion, and I was so disappointed to learn there were no such places anymore. People don't learn to read the ancient words unless they're a witch or a ranger. According to the Witch, the godsmen discourage reading, blaming the knowledge of words for the fall of the cities and the humbling of the people.

"What you'd call magic is more about the way we can hear each other in our heads. 'Telepathy' was the old word for it. And a scant few of us have dreams and visions. We *see* things that happened, and what might happen too. But Moran didn't know any of this, and so my threat worked. Besides, I'd just have given Sari a tincture to add to his meals to give him a bad case of limp cock for a moon or so. And then I'd have asked him for another fee to cure him."

Gerry laughed in earnest. "Is this what you learned from the Witch? Extorting fees?"

Ghost wrapped his arms around Gerry's waist. "Don't be silly. Besides, the Witch was much better at this sort of thing. She got a new drying shed for not cursing someone once."

"Wicked." Gerry leaned in to kiss Ghost, lingering over Ghost's full lips. "Did the Witch play this game often?"

"Only when someone was simply too big an ass to understand anything else," Ghost replied and stretched up for another kiss.

The wail of the baby interrupted them, and Gerry looked at Ghost with a sigh.

"Sometimes I'm truly glad we can't make a babe," Gerry admitted. "Do you need to go help?"

"Sari's still weak enough, so I should," Ghost replied. "Don't go anywhere. I'm not quite finished with what you started."

Chapter Two

THE SUMMER PASSED quickly, and autumn nipped the air most mornings. Gerry hunted more frequently, smoking what he could to preserve the meat for the coming winter. Ghost wrapped root vegetables in straw and filled the cool cellar with sealed clay jars of preserves and small casks of lamp oil. Gerry chopped wood and stacked it to dry while Ghost aired out the woolen clothing and extra blankets they would need.

Gerry put aside a few choice sind pelts to make a warm cloak for Ghost for the winter. The lithe predators were already sporting their winter coats with the heavy undercoat that insulated them from cold and snow. He kept the thick, tawny fur on the inside and dyed the leather outside a deep green. He spent close to a full moon preparing the pelts and joining them with tiny, strong stitches. The finished cloak was a luxurious gift, and Gerry was eager to see his beautiful Ghost wearing it.

The day he finished the cloak, Gerry stopped Ghost in the main room as Ghost was headed to the yard. The late afternoon sun caught Ghost's spiral as Gerry shook out the cloak. Ghost stood frozen, with eyes wide and mouth agape as Gerry hung the garment around his shoulders to test the fit.

The cloak looked even better on Ghost than Gerry hoped, the green of the leather a deeper shade than Ghost's shimmering peridot spiral. Gerry waited for Ghost's words, admiring the sight of his beloved mate.

"This...this is the most exquisite thing I've ever seen. I can't believe you made a cloak for me. It's too much, love."

Gerry laughed, delighted by Ghost's reaction. He loved to pamper Ghost, not simply to prove he was a proper alpha, but because Ghost was so unaccustomed to being pampered. Gerry leaned in to kiss Ghost and revel in the joy on Ghost's face. Ghost returned the kiss with great fervor. Gerry tugged up the hood as he kissed Ghost, the soft golden fur tickling Gerry's forehead.

"I want you to be warm this winter. You'll get called out for all sorts of emergencies. People dropping firewood on their toes and getting icicles stuck on their noses. Everyone will want my witch to make them better." Gerry nibbled soft kisses as he teased Ghost, watching Ghost's pale eyes light up. "So I have to make sure my witch stays warm and healthy, and since I can't keep you in bed with me all winter, this is the next best thing."

Ghost ducked his head. "You say such things. I'm sure there won't be people coming with icicles on their noses."

"No," Gerry agreed, his arms firm around Ghost. "If they're smart, they'll be in bed. Bundled up and making new babes for you to deliver come the harvest. You'll be running from house to house trying to make sure everyone is all right."

Ghost laughed. "Then I'll make you follow me around with a bucket of hot water and a big pile of linens. You can be my apprentice." He reached up to push the hood back. "I should put this away until the weather gets cold. I don't want it to get ruined."

Gerry helped Ghost take off the cloak. He draped the garment over a chair and reached for the laces on Ghost's linen tunic.

"What are you doing?" Ghost asked, his hands darting up to cover Gerry's hands.

"Well, taking off your cloak put me in mind to take off a few more encumbrances. Like this tunic, and your boots, and your breeches." Gerry untied the laces and started to lift the hem of Ghost's tunic.

"What if someone comes?" Ghost raised his arms anyway.

"We close the door." Gerry tugged off Ghost's tunic and crossed the room to do just that. He strolled back over, watching the color rise in Ghost's cheeks. Ghost's blush was not the only thing rising, and Gerry smirked when he saw Ghost had already toed off his boots.

Gerry reached down, lifting Ghost up until his legs wrapped around Gerry's hips. Ghost's arms draped over Gerry's shoulders and around his neck.

"Moon shine on me, Ghost, when you look at me like this," Gerry murmured, carrying Ghost toward their bedroom.

"You talk too much," Ghost said and leaned in, offering a kiss to Gerry.

Gerry took the offer and plundered Ghost's mouth. He eased Ghost onto the bed, kneeling on the thick mattress as he leaned forward. He supported himself with one arm, the other behind him to push at his own boots. Ghost's fingers made quick work of the laces of Gerry's tunic. Gerry paused for a brief moment to marvel at the way Ghost could go from shy and innocent to eager and wanton in an instant. He had been Ghost's first lover, Ghost's only lover. The meek apprentice hiding in the shadows had vanished as Ghost's confidence had grown, until now when Ghost was comfortable enough to revel in their lovemaking.

Ghost tugged at Gerry's tunic, pushing it up over Gerry's ribs. Gerry wriggled his free arm out of the sleeve. A puff of air hit Gerry's lips as Ghost laughed into the kiss, and

Gerry felt a nip on his lower lip. He pulled away and peered into Ghost's sparkling blue eyes. Joy and heated passion reflected back at him as Ghost pulled the tunic over Gerry's head with a firm tug and tossed it aside.

Gerry knelt between Ghost's parted thighs and ran his gaze over Ghost's smooth and slender torso, relishing the way Ghost's pink nipples had hardened. He reached up to tease one, watching Ghost's eyelids flutter in response to the touch. Gerry leaned in to kiss Ghost's inviting lips again.

Ghost's deft fingers pulled the laces of Gerry's breeches loose while Gerry explored Ghost's willing mouth. Ghost slid Gerry's breeches past his hips, allowing Gerry's hard cock to spring free.

"Ghost," Gerry breathed, watching as Ghost unraveled the tangle of his own laces and lifted his pert rear to slide the soft leather over the curve of his cheeks. Gerry shifted to let Ghost kick off the breeches and then Ghost spread his pale thighs in welcome.

Gerry stood for a moment to peel off the last of his clothes, his cock proud as he kicked the leather aside. He scrabbled in the basket on the table by the bed, finding the small vial of oil they kept there. He raised a brow in inquiry, and Ghost nodded.

"Not a lot," Ghost said, and Gerry's pulse raced at the husky note in his voice. "I want to feel you, love."

Gerry's cock jumped in response to Ghost's request, and he dribbled a few drops of oil on his fingers. He spread the oil over Ghost's entrance, feeling the tight hole quiver and relax as he worked the oil in. Gerry breached Ghost with one finger and worked a little more of the oil in as Ghost let out a wanton gasp. Desire brightened Ghost's eyes and made his exotic looks even more beguiling. Gerry leaned down to drag his tongue over Ghost's pink nipple as he thrust a second finger into Ghost.

The way Ghost responded never failed to arouse Gerry. As often as he made love to Ghost, it still took Gerry's breath away when Ghost was this eager. Gerry had claimed his Ghost for the first time in a ruined city, in front of a campfire. He had always felt their initial lovemaking had lacked a certain propriety, due in large part to the dead ranger nearby. He had been striving to make up for it ever since, and Ghost had been a willing participant.

"You're thinking again." Ghost's raspy voice startled Gerry from his thoughts. Ghost buried his fingers in Gerry's hair and tugged. "I'm ready enough. I don't want to wait."

"You're sure, beloved?" Gerry asked, but he was already moving, his fingers sliding out of Ghost. He could not resist the urge to bury himself in Ghost and feel the slick, tight heat surrounding his cock. Gerry took a moment to rub his oiled fingers over the shaft of his cock, precome smearing as his fingers slid over the swollen head.

Ghost's answer was pure Ghost. His legs wrapped around Gerry's hips, pulling Gerry down, and Gerry gasped a laugh as he grabbed his cock to line the head up with Ghost's loosened hole.

"I don't want to wait," Ghost said again. He cried out as Gerry breached him, the swollen head of Gerry's cock pushing past the slight resistance Ghost's hole offered.

Gerry moaned in pleasure as the firm passage engulfed his cock. Ghost's muscles tightened around him as he sank farther into the inviting heat.

"Moon shine on me, Ghost," Gerry rasped. "You feel so good. How do you always manage to be this tight?" He groaned as he pressed in until he could go no farther, his balls snug against the warmth of Ghost's round cheeks. He paused for a moment, wanting to give Ghost a chance to adjust, as Ghost trembled beneath him. "Tell me when to move, beloved."

Ghost made a small noise that Gerry could not interpret and lifted his hips a little more. The movement dragged a gasp from Ghost, and Gerry could feel Ghost clench around his cock, the pressure rippling along the shaft.

Gerry felt moisture against his belly, and he looked down to see the precome welling from Ghost's cock, the head a dusky rose against the shaft. Gerry looked into Ghost's lust-darkened eyes.

"So good," Ghost whispered. "Move, love. I need you to move now."

Ghost's hands caressed Gerry's ribs and wrapped around Gerry's back. He pushed his hips up and rubbed his cock against the muscles of Gerry's abdomen. Gerry felt the pulse of the vein along the underside of Ghost's cock. He hissed when Gerry began to move, and Gerry paused until Ghost nodded.

Gerry kept the pace steady at first, letting Ghost continue to adjust. He always worried Ghost would push for too much, too soon, and no matter how often they made love, Gerry insisted on a slow start. He could tell Ghost was getting impatient, though. Ghost's fingers dug into Gerry's back, and Ghost's legs tightened around his hips.

"Fierce little thing," Gerry teased, a little breathless as he moved faster, his thrusts deeper. He was rewarded with a yelp as Ghost matched the accelerated pace, eyelids fluttering closed. Ghost's glossy white hair spread out across the thick quilt, and a few tendrils clung to Ghost's damp skin. Gerry's balls grew heavy, and he leaned close to whisper to Ghost. "Touch yourself for me, my precious Ghost."

Ghost's eyes flew open, and his teeth gleamed as he caught his lower lip between them, but he managed a nod as he looked up at Gerry. Ghost's hand slipped between them and wrapped around his own cock. He moaned as he tugged, the strokes ragged.

Neither one of them was going to last much longer. Ghost's tight passage gripped Gerry's cock with more insistence, his balls drawing up. Ghost was all but painting his belly with precome, trembling beneath Gerry.

Ghost whimpered and let go of his cock, his hand sliding under Gerry's arm, scrabbling against Gerry's back. He shifted and howled, and Gerry felt Ghost spasm around his cock almost hard enough to be painful as the heat of Ghost's come spattered between them.

Ghost's fingers dug into the muscles of Gerry's back and Gerry's orgasm erupted. White light flooded Gerry's vision, and he cried out, beyond words as he ground into Ghost, his come pumping out in eager spurts. Ghost tensed even more beneath him for a moment before relaxing and collapsing to the down-filled mattress in a boneless heap.

The wild pounding of his own heart thundered in Gerry's ears as he struggled to catch his breath. Ghost was breathing almost as hard, hands now flat against Gerry's back. Ghost's legs loosened and lowered past Gerry's hips, a faint tremor running through the long muscles of Ghost's thighs. The movement caused Ghost's hole to grip Gerry's cock, and it was Gerry's turn to tremble with sated bliss.

"Next time," Gerry said, his voice hoarse. "You're on top."

The joke earned Gerry a ragged little chuckle, and Ghost wriggled. "Getting lazy?" Ghost teased as his fingers danced upward to trace the bones of Gerry's shoulder.

"Worn out. My mate is insatiable. He never lets me rest." Gerry got one elbow underneath him and propped himself up. He looked down at Ghost, feeling a powerful upswelling of love.

"How terrible," Ghost said and tilted his face, inviting a kiss. "Poor, poor man. Let me kiss it and make it better."

"Isn't this how we started?" Gerry said, and he laughed when Ghost pinched his upper arm. He leaned in to kiss Ghost's facetious pout. "Mm, yes, seems familiar."

Gerry held Ghost and kissed him, enjoying the sweet aftermath. He reached up to caress the spiral of peridot shining against Ghost's forehead, and Ghost smiled and moved closer. "Your mark's been quiet," Gerry said. He let his finger trail off down Ghost's temple and past Ghost's cheekbone to trace Ghost's full lips, still kiss swollen and plump. "No visions?"

"Not lately, and don't call them down on me," Ghost said. "The Seeker is biding her time, I think, but I'll take the peace while I can." He looked up at Gerry with a smile loving enough to melt Gerry's heart.

"Then we'll talk about something else," Gerry agreed. "What do you want to do for the rest of the day?"

Ghost was thoughtful for a moment. "Do you have any more surprises for me to try on?"

When the words sank in, Gerry let out a laugh and grabbed Ghost in a tight hug. The sudden movement made Gerry's cock slip free and earned a mewl of disappointment from Ghost. Gerry muffled the protest with a kiss.

THE MOON WAS high in the night sky when Ghost woke, his heart pounding. Gerry's arms were around him, the warmth of Gerry's breath against his ear. Ghost forced his muscles to relax and then concentrated on calming his racing heart. The spiral heated and his stomach churned.

Ghost untangled himself from Gerry and managed to slip free. He got out of their bed and shivered in the crisp night air. He snatched a small blanket from the chest against the wall to drape around his shoulders and went out to the washhouse, his bare feet making no sound as he walked over the slate path. The moon was near as bright as day, and Ghost paused to gaze up at the silver disc. He sensed the pressure behind his forehead, marking one of the Seeker's sendings.

Ghost hurried to relieve himself and was on his way back to the house when the pressure behind the spiral rose to a sharp, stabbing pain. He lifted his face to the moon, clutched the blanket tight, and let the images fill him. He had no other option. When the Seeker touched him, Ghost had no choice but to *see*.

The vision was the usual jumble of fleeting images and muffled sounds with an obscure message. An urgent sense of dread accompanied the images, far stronger than any message the Seeker had ever sent him. Ghost knew better than to look for any meaning while he was flooded with the initial barrage. He would remember, as he always did, and he could sort it out later.

Ghost stood transfixed on the slate path, enduring the pain and listening to the message only he could hear. The chill of the pavers traveled up through his bare feet. A strange clicking sound baffled him. Before Ghost could try to figure it out, comforting warmth surrounded him. He turned his head with care, trying to clear away the images filling his head. Gerry's strong arm was around Ghost's shoulders, and Ghost leaned into his mate with a grateful sigh.

"Ghost, what are you doing out here? You're freezing, and your teeth are chattering. Your spiral. Did you have a vision?"

"I was on my way back from the washhouse." Ghost lifted his shoulders a scant bit. "I looked up at the moon, and I just *saw*. How long was I out here?"

Gerry guided him back to the house, his sturdy arm a bastion of safety for Ghost. "I have no idea. I woke up and you weren't there. I rolled over and saw you out the window. You were standing still as a statue, and your spiral was glowing bright. I put the kettle on the hearth and came out for you."

Once in the house, Gerry made Ghost sit on the bench by the hearth. The kettle was steaming already, and Ghost relaxed even more in the welcome warmth of the kitchen.

"I didn't mean to scare you," Ghost said. "I'm sorry."

"How were you to know you'd have a vision?" Gerry poured hot water over the tea, and the fragrance filled Ghost's nose. "Do you want to talk about what you *saw*?"

Ghost had not expected the offer, and he looked at Gerry in surprise. "You know, no one has ever asked me to talk about my visions before. They're infrequent and the Witch never asked about them. I didn't make an effort to share them with her either. She's not a seer, and she doesn't understand what the visions are like or how much *seeing* can hurt."

Gerry poured them each a cup of hot tea and sat on the bench next to Ghost, his comforting arm returning to Ghost's shoulders. "I didn't know if you were allowed to talk about them," Gerry said. "This is the first vision you've had since we've been a family. Nightmares, yes, but no visions."

"I'm sorry about those too." Ghost would have continued, but Gerry put a finger to Ghost's lips.

"Don't apologize. You've had a few nightmares, and you were entitled to be upset, after being kidnapped like you were. I thought I'd lost you, and I've had a few bad nights too." Gerry pulled Ghost closer. "We're mates. We're there for each other, and we don't have to apologize for needing a little support and comfort."

"I'm still working on remembering. I know I can ask you for what I need. I'm still not used to having anyone, though." Ghost relaxed into Gerry's embrace, the warmth of Gerry's body and the heat of the tea banishing the last of the shivering. "But I'd like to talk about the vision, if you don't mind. Talking might help me decipher the meaning." Gerry nodded, and Ghost continued in a soft voice.

"A vision's never really clear, you know. I get this jumbled-up mess of pictures and sounds. The only clear part is usually a sentence or two, more like a riddle than anything else. I have to figure out what the whole thing means and, hopefully, not screw up whatever it is I'm supposed to do." Ghost slid his fingers into his hair and tugged the strands as he tried to remember.

"The vision started with an image of a child. A boy...or maybe a girl. The child might have been the Witch seen from a distance? I don't know. The child turned, opened its mouth to speak, and blood poured out. The vision shifted to a furious winter scene. Everything flew by so fast. A howling, twisting wind was thrashing the snow and trees all about, making it difficult to tell what I was *seeing*. I think I *saw* stones carved with witchmarks in the snow, though."

Ghost frowned as he tried to concentrate on the images, but instead, he kept coming up with the sounds. "The sounds were awful. A desperate, choking sound. Do you remember the Highsummer feast, when Torrance's family got so sick? Someone used one or two of the wrong mushrooms, and they all vomited to the point of exhaustion. The sound I heard precisely matched the awful sound of their retching."

Gerry's eyes were wide, and Ghost felt a little sorry for having shared this particular bit with him. But Gerry had asked, and Ghost did not want to lie to him. Ghost was still learning about dealing with people, but he had figured out very quickly the truth was always the best way.

"And the riddle?" Gerry asked.

"So odd. A female voice, but I might have thought so because I was expecting the Seeker." Ghost sipped the hot tea. "The voice said, 'What was known is lost. What is lost must be found. What is found is the way home,' which sounds incredibly ominous and difficult."

"I don't want to think about anything ominous. We did ominous once. Isn't once enough?" Gerry said, and Ghost wanted to assuage the worry in his eyes.

"The vision will probably turn out to be something completely innocuous," Ghost said. "Visions are awkward. The worse the riddle sounds, the more likely it'll be nothing big. The simple ones scare me more because those always turn out badly. Like the vision I had before I met you. 'One who leads, one who loves, one who is known by the—'" He broke off before uttering the dreaded name of the Eighth. "Well, you know the rest. You showed up in Mother's arms, with a broken leg and a pouting Conn tagging along. I thought the vision was about the three of you, but I was wrong. You were the one who led and the one who loved. Bernd was the last part."

"I don't want to think about him, or that night," Gerry said, his voice firm. "Not as though I wouldn't do it all over again to protect you. But I've never killed anyone before, and to be honest, I hope I never have to kill a person again. I can kill a runner, or a sind. Hunting for meat and pelts is fine, as long as you make a clean kill and never take more than you can use. But when I killed him, I felt cold inside. I thought I'd never get warm again."

Ghost looked up at Gerry and shook his head. "I don't want to kill anyone either. And you're right. Let's not think about the past. I'm feeling a lot warmer. The tea really helped. You take such good care of me, love."

"I'm glad, beloved." Gerry took Ghost's cup and went over to the deep stone tub where they washed the dishes. He set the cups in the wooden bucket of water and moved the kettle away from the hearth.

To Ghost, it appeared Gerry was trying to keep busy, perhaps to avoid talking. Ghost stood up, grabbing at the blanket before it slid off his shoulders. He walked over to Gerry and embraced his mate from behind, his hands flat against Gerry's sculpted abdomen.

"Don't keep it all locked inside," Ghost said, his voice soft. "I may not have much experience interacting with people, but I know how harmful keeping worry inside can be. I'd feel a lot better if you came out and said what's on your mind."

Gerry turned around, and Ghost thought the smile Gerry wore looked far too sad to be a real smile. Gerry pulled the blanket up higher around Ghost's shoulders.

"We need to get you something warmer for middle-of-the-night trips to the washhouse this winter," Gerry said, and he brushed Ghost's hair back from his face. "I was thinking about what happened. Killing a person shouldn't have been so easy. No one said I did wrong to kill the bastard. Bernd." Gerry spat the name. "Not Mother, not the Witch, no one. The elders had nothing to say. They were quick to give me permission to establish myself as an alpha, with you as my dependent."

Ghost listened, hearing the question Gerry was not quite asking. He had to bite back a smile when he realized this was what the Witch used to do to him. She had always answered the question Ghost had not been brave enough to ask. When he was small, he used to think she could hear his thoughts.

"Bernd had killed before and he'd have killed again," Ghost said. "Murder wasn't hard for him. He was crazy enough to be exiled from the rangers, and the truth is most rangers have no problem taking another person's life to begin with. They live in the wilder places, where there aren't elders and alphas to make order. The one thing they truly fear is death, and the witches use their fear against them." Ghost held tight to Gerry, hearing Gerry's heart beating and feeling the steady rise and fall of Gerry's breathing against his cheek.

"But you're not like him. You're a good alpha and a good man. You'd rather find a way to deal with problems by talking instead of resorting to violence. Your restraint is more than what you were taught by Mother. It's also what's in your heart and why I fell in love with you."

Ghost took a deep breath. He still felt uncomfortable speaking earnestly and directly to people, even with Gerry. He always expected to be rebuffed and told he did not understand.

Ghost tensed when Gerry spoke. "For someone who thinks he's not adept at dealing with people, you've got a way of getting right to the heart of the matter." Gerry pulled Ghost closer and held him tight for a moment. "Thank you, for believing in me and for thinking I'm a good man. Now, let's go to bed and try to sleep before the sun wakes us."

Ghost let Gerry guide him to their bedroom, where Ghost folded the blanket before he crawled back under the warm quilt. The quilt had been a parting gift from the Witch, thick and downy, the fabric still bright and sturdy. Ghost had sheltered under the quilt when he was small. He was comforted by this piece of his past each night, and he wondered if the Witch had woven protections into the very stitches of the quilt. A silly thought, but Ghost found it as reassuring as Gerry's arms around him. Ghost rested his head on Gerry's warm shoulder. The vibrations of Gerry's gentle, regular snoring calmed Ghost and sent him off into a dreamless sleep.

Chapter Three

HARVESTTIDE HAD COME and gone already. The days were noticeably shorter, and the leaves fell in drifts of scarlet and gold. The door stood open anyway, despite a crisp breeze.

"Bright day?" The voice was female and tentative, the greeting turned into a question.

Ghost looked up from his formulary cabinet. Moran had built it with commendable speed and care within a moon after Sari delivered. "Lady smile on you," Ghost replied. "What brings you?"

He finished making the notation in the ancient words, placed the pottery jar back in the proper niche, and turned around to face the woman.

"Oh!" Her eyes widened as she took in Ghost. "They said your mark was all bright jewels and not made with inks, but you know I thought it gossip." She ducked her head a little. "But my business with you, good witch, yes. I came about my old dam. She's been poorly, and I'm at my wits' end."

"Can you tell me a little about what's wrong?" Ghost asked, trying to keep his voice mild. The woman seemed as jumpy as a sind who had scented the hunters.

"Of course." She tugged at her thick shawl, her fingers plucking at the edges. "My dam was always busy, in spite of her age, but the past quarter moon she's been getting tired too easy. I woke on Ladyday, and she was still in her bed. She shooed me off, said it was only age. Not two days later, she was vomiting up her tea and bread, and her head was hot as hearthstones. She seemed a bit better Moonday, but then she was back to it."

The woman shook her head. "I nursed my own babes through all sorts of little upsets, like when they ate something they shouldn't have. But this is different, good witch. My alpha says no, but she's my dam. I can't sit by. He's a good one, my alpha, most of the time. He took my dam in when my sire passed over, and never a word of complaint about another mouth. But he thinks I'm fretting over nothing, while my dam is getting weaker."

Ghost nodded in agreement. "Give me a moment to pack my supplies, and I'll come along with you." He moved the stew to the edge of the hearth and took his Seeker's kiss from the drawer of his formulary cabinet. The device was fed and ready, and he placed it into a small leather pouch, along with two pottery jars.

"Do you have a name?" Ghost asked, trying to set the nervous woman at ease. He took a short woolen cloak from a peg by the door, and the woman clucked her tongue.

"I'm Mai, and my dam is Merrah," the woman said, and she reached out to finger his cloak. "I weave, good witch. Will you take a proper cloak for your fee?"

Ghost smiled at Mai's unspoken assessment of his cloak. The garment was old and not so warm anymore, but the weather had not yet turned cold enough to justify the gorgeous fur cloak Gerry had made for him. "Let's see what I can do for your dam first," he suggested. "A cloak's a high fee if I can do nothing to heal her."

Mai lowered her head again and led Ghost down the path to the village. She kept sneaking glances at him sidelong, and Ghost found himself more amused than annoyed to see her shy interest. As far as Ghost knew, he was the only person from the Northlands in the village, and he was well aware he was a curiosity. He was getting used to the looks, much like the village was getting used to its new witch.

Mai lived in a small house well off the main market street. The step was swept, and the kitchen appeared tidy and welcoming, but Ghost could smell the sickness as soon as he walked in. He looked over at Mai, and she gestured to the back of the house.

"Merrah's room is this way." Mai walked ahead, raising her voice to call out, "Merrah, I'm back. I've brought the witch to see you." She looked back at Ghost. "She was awake when I left, but I'm always worried the fever will make her forget things."

"I've forgotten nothing, child."

The voice was old but firm. Mai opened the door to let Ghost step into the bedroom. The smell of illness was worse here, although the aged woman in the bed appeared clean, and her hair was neatly braided down her back. Dark eyes as bright as a bird's looked at Ghost with open curiosity.

"When did witches turn into young men?" Merrah asked. "I'm not complaining, mind you. But where did the little girl go? Off wandering again?"

Ghost needed a moment to realize Merrah was referring to the Witch, and he could not help a small, surprised laugh. "She left, yes. She didn't say where she was going." He could judge the toll the days of illness had taken on Merrah. Her wrinkled skin was papery and dry, and she appeared far too weak for his liking.

Ghost reached out to rest his hand on Merrah's forehead, heat coming off her in waves. "Have you kept anything in your stomach at all today?"

Merrah made a small noise and shook her head, not lifting it from the pile of pillows that propped her up. "The child here brings me weak tea and broth on a regular basis, and I eat for her but they come back up as fast as they go down. The truth is, little witch, I'm too tired to keep trying."

Ghost looked at Merrah, hearing the exhaustion and surrender in her voice. "The Witch named me Ghost. Will you try a little longer, for me? At least let me *see* what I can tell, and perhaps I can give you some relief." He waited for the feeble nod and placed both hands on either side of Merrah's face. He watched her eyes widen just a little, and he knew she was looking at the spiral stones on his forehead flaring to life as he tried to *see* below the surface.

The illness was elusive, not an ordinary stomach flux at all. The malady was not tied to what was eaten, and the fever was wound around the stomach disorder in a way Ghost had never seen. He felt the increased warmth against his forehead, and he tried to look a little deeper, but whatever this illness was, it skittered just past where he could *see*.

Ghost let go of Merrah and turned his head to Mai. "Do you think you could warm some water? I have something I'd like to try. First, I want to do something about this fever."

Ghost opened his pouch and took out the Seeker's kiss. He twisted the tube until he heard two clicks and turned to Merrah.

"This will sting a bit, but the serum goes right to the fever and the soreness." Ghost waited for the tired nod that gave him leave to proceed, and he pressed the glowing top of the Seeker's kiss, the tip against Merrah's arm. Merrah did not even flinch, but she closed her eyes and Ghost could see the tension at the corners of her mouth ease.

"Rest a moment and I'll make an infusion for you." Ghost stood, putting the Seeker's kiss back in his pouch. "Don't give up, Merrah. Mai needs you for a while yet." He felt the tingling behind his spiral, and he heard the ring of truth in his words. "There'll be a time to rest, but this isn't the time."

Merrah did not open her eyes, but she chuckled, a dry rasp in her throat. "You're as bad as the little girl who left. She liked a drop of blood, though. You've got kinder hands." She lifted her own thin and wrinkled hand from the bed. "Go make your tisane with the child. I'll stay."

Ghost left the bedroom, already reaching in his pouch for the two pottery jars. In the kitchen, Mai's shoulders hunched inward as she heated the water. She did not turn around, and Ghost realized she was weeping.

He was never sure how to comfort someone, and Ghost stood still for a moment. The Witch had rarely offered an embrace, leaving Ghost with little in the way of an example. All he had to rely on was instinct and what he had learned from the comfort of Gerry's arms. He placed the pottery jars on the scrubbed table and touched Mai's shoulder, hesitant.

Mai turned, her face wet with tears. She stepped into Ghost's arms, put her face into his shoulder, and shook with silent sobs. Ghost held her, just a little awkward, making soft noises he hoped would soothe the grieving woman. He let her weep for a time before he spoke.

"I'm not sure what this illness is. I know what's happening to her, and I will do what I can for the symptoms, but I don't know the why of the malady." Ghost paused, patting Mai's back with a gentle hand. "The Seeker's kiss will help with the fever and aches. The infusion will settle her stomach and also help the fever. Once she's managed to keep down two cups of the mixture, she can have broth and bland foods. Eggs cooked soft, if you have them."

Mai's voice was barely a whisper. "Thank you, Ghost. You're very kind. It means more to me than I can say." Her voice nearly broke, and she turned to reach for a clean cup, taking a ragged breath. "Show me what to do for her."

Ghost patted Mai's shoulder. "This jar, with the blue wax. One pinch, like this." He pinched the herbs between his thumb and first finger and sprinkled the crushed leaves in the cup. "This is for the fever, mostly. The jar with the red wax is for the stomach. The infusion's going to be strong, but with a little honey, it will taste pretty good. Two pinches of this one and then the hot water. Let the cup sit until you can smell the herbs, and add a little honey."

"Merrah doesn't like food to be too sweet, and she takes her drinks good and hot," Mai said. "So, let's bring this medicine to her and see if she can keep it down."

Ghost let Mai carry the infusion, and he watched as she held the cup for Merrah, her manner tender and loving as she fed her dam small sips until the cup was empty. Ghost could see the tension in Mai's shoulders. A clean bucket and soft cloth sat nearby in case Merrah needed to purge. But the moments passed, and Merrah leaned back against the pillows.

Mai looked over her shoulder and gave Ghost a tiny smile. She turned back to Merrah and smoothed the blanket over the old woman. "You feel cooler," Mai said. She took one wrinkled hand between her own two hands.

"The medicine's sitting easy, child," Merrah said. "The drink wasn't too nasty, either." She looked up at Ghost with her bright bird's eyes. "A male witch. Such wonders I've seen with these old eyes. Now go, and fuss over someone who really needs you, little Ghost."

Mai smiled, much stronger this time. "You're worth fussing over, and you know so, Merrah. You've fussed enough over me and my babes too. Now's my turn." She stroked the old woman's hand before she stood. "I'll see Ghost out and I'll be back."

At the door, Mai appeared relieved. "Thank you. Truly. If she can keep the medicine down and another dose in a while, I'll give her some broth. I'll get eggs for her too. Will you stop back and see her?"

"I will," Ghost promised. "I'll stop tomorrow after high sun. But if you need me sooner, come for me."

THE FOLLOWING AFTERNOON, Mai told Ghost how Merrah had managed broth the night before and soft-cooked eggs this morning. The fever was down and Merrah's color was better. Ghost was no closer to knowing why Merrah had fallen ill, but relieving the symptoms seemed to help her start to mend. Ghost left after telling Mai to keep up the infusion three times daily until she ran out of herbs and to come for him if Merrah took a bad turn. Mai would be quick enough to come, he decided. Ghost was gratified to have been of help, even if he had only treated the symptoms.

A pang of longing and an urgent need to see Gerry overcame Ghost, and he quickened his pace to get home. As he passed the old oak tree marking the entrance to the market street, a shrill scream from a house to his right drew his attention. He ran to the building without stopping to think and pushed open the door.

A young woman bent over an elderly man lying supine on the floor of the kitchen. Ghost needed no more than a glance to see the man was dead, his lips already blue beneath smears of dried blood. The house reeked of illness, and the young woman who sobbed over him appeared disheveled and exhausted. She looked up at Ghost, her eyes focused on the spiral of stones on his forehead.

"He was fine. He was fine!" She sobbed and clutched the dead man's tunic. "He had a fever, and he vomited, but he was getting better. I was sure of it. Then he started to vomit again, blood this time. I don't know why he got up. I heard the crash. It's not fair! He was fine!"

Ghost reached down to lift her to her feet. "Hush, come away. He was your alpha?"

"I don't know what will happen to me now. I don't know what to do," the young woman sobbed.

"The elders will decide," Ghost replied, feeling awkward in the face of her storm of tears. He looked around at the untidy kitchen, wondering if this chaos was normal or if the young woman had been overwhelmed by caring for the elderly man. "I'll ask my alpha to speak with them on your behalf. What was his name?"

The young woman seemed baffled by Ghost's question. "I need to get him off the floor. He doesn't belong down there. The stones are too cold for him." She dropped to her knees again, and her hands fluttered over the body.

"Let me help you," Ghost insisted. "I can carry him to his room if that's what you want. Do you want me to get someone to take him to be buried for you?"

"No, leave him. I'll call the guard," she said, a fresh sob shaking her shoulders. "I'll take care of him. Thank you, good witch."

Ghost turned to leave, but her soft voice stopped him. "If I had called you, would he have lived?"

Ghost sighed. "I don't know. Why do you want to add such weight to your grief?"

"Because I thought about coming for you and I didn't. He said he was fine." Her sobs broke out again and Ghost paused.

"I don't know if I should leave you like this," he admitted, wondering if he was missing some subtle signal. "Is there anyone who can help you?"

She shook her head. "Half this street is down with the vomiting and fever. Mostly the older ones and the littlest ones. Hasn't anyone come to you about the sick?"

Ghost was taken aback by her words. "What do you mean? How many people have fallen ill?" A curious pressure warmed his spiral, not quite the push of a vision, but more than the mild tiredness from having exerted his abilities for Merrah's sake.

"I don't know. I haven't gotten out in the past two days. I was so tired, and he was better. I was trying to rest. And then the new vomiting started." Her forlorn voice drew Ghost back to her side.

"I saw Merrah. Mai's dam. Do you know her?" Ghost asked.

"I do. Did she have this? The fever and the purging and then the bloody vomiting?"

Ghost's thoughts were racing. He had heard tell of illnesses that could spring up out of nowhere and spread like wildfire, leaving far too many dead in their wake. The prospect of losing his village to a virulent outbreak made Ghost's stomach clench. He straightened up, looking down at the girl. "Merrah had fever and purging but not the bloody vomit. What about you? Were you ill?"

She peered up at Ghost, red-eyed and teary. "I felt poorly for a day and purged a few times, but then I was well again. What does it mean?"

"I don't know yet. I need to leave and find out what's happening. I'll come back in the morning to check on you. I want to make sure you don't get sick like your alpha. Will you be all right staying here?"

The girl ducked her head and stood, moving as though she ached all over. "I have nowhere else to go."

"I'll talk to my alpha. We'll make sure you have a place. Gerry can speak for you with the elders, and he'll be glad to help."

"Go find out, because there's too many getting sick now. He was fine, I know it. This shouldn't have happened to him. He was a good alpha." The girl's haunted eyes tore at Ghost's heart. "He was all I knew."

THE GIRL WAS right. Half the street was sickened by whatever this was, and three others in addition to her alpha had succumbed. Ghost hastened home because his Seeker's kiss needed to be fed, and he was going to have to prepare a great deal more of the healing herbs for those who had just become ill. For the very old and the very young who had reached the bloody vomiting stage, he could do little beyond making them comfortable. It was the Seeker's will if they survived or went into the arms of her dread mate.

Ghost was glad to see Gerry was already home. As much as he needed the comfort and normalcy of Gerry's arms around him, he waved Gerry off. "I've been dealing with an outbreak of something," Ghost said. "Four have died already and a hand more are close to death. I want to change my clothing and wash before I let you near me. I don't know enough about this illness to know if I can pass it to you, and I won't take a chance."

Gerry's eyes widened, but he stepped away. "Do you want to eat? Something simple so you can get to bed and rest."

Ghost shook his head and spoke quickly. "I have to measure out more herbs, so I won't be sleeping any time soon. I need to check the market for ginger root tomorrow too. I know I'm running low and ginger helps settle the stomach."

"You won't do anyone any good if you're exhausted," Gerry replied, but Ghost was already on his way to the washhouse with his cloak and tunic in his hands.

Ghost finished stripping in the warmth of the washhouse, the bed of coals beside the copper tub keeping the water warm. He wet himself down and reached for the soap he had made from the large nuts Gerry called conkers. The Witch had called them "aesculus hippocastanum" in the ancient words. The bars were rough and scoured away grime and dead skin. Ghost was thorough as he scrubbed, mindful of the Witch's lectures on washing after treating an outbreak of anything. Ghost took great care to follow her advice. Such caution had served the Witch well, after all.

As he scrubbed, Ghost considered whether or not he should use the scrying mirror, as the Witch had taught him, to consult with other witches about this contagion. A flux of the stomach was not uncommon, nor was a fever. To have them together usually meant the person had eaten something that was spoiled, but the illness resolved in all save the weakest. The bloody vomit was what bothered Ghost. Hemorrhage was not a common symptom at all. Another witch might have encountered a similar case and could help him figure this out.

If this was a plague of some sort, disaster was sure to follow. Harvesttide was past, but the weather was still warm enough to ensure the market was lively. The last few caravans from the South were rolling in, the drays pulling heavy wagons laden with exotic treats that would have to last until the weather allowed for trade to resume. Trade always brought the whole village together, and contagion could pass from person to person fast enough to make containing any outbreak impossible.

Contacting the witchsisters meant exposing himself to the witches who did not approve of him, though, and Ghost was not eager to endure another round of their venom. He had passed all manner of tests and had done everything he could to prove he would honor the laws of the sisterhood. His ability to *see*, which was spoken of in the most ancient texts, should have been an asset. Yet some of the more resistant witches had used his talent as a seer as an excuse to speak against him. "Abomination" was the preferred insult, and the word still rankled.

But in the end, Ghost was a healer, and his obligation was to the sick. His own feelings and sensibilities needed to be put aside. He decided he would give himself this night and one more day to look for answers himself. If he was still uncertain, he would turn to the sisterhood and let those few witches who hated him have their say. He was seeking help for his patients and his village, making his behavior proper for any witch. If they could find fault with him for seeking help, they would look foolish, not him.

Satisfied with his decision, Ghost sluiced away the thin lather with the dipper. He realized he had forgotten to bring a towel with him. Putting his soiled clothing back on was out of the question. Ghost resigned himself to a quick and chilly run back to the house, naked and wet.

"Sea take me for getting lost in my head again," Ghost muttered, turning around to grab his boots, at least, before he made his dash to the kitchen. He gasped as a thick towel wrapped around him. He turned to see Gerry standing behind him.

"You were so busy thinking about what you needed to do. I watched you walk off with no towel, no clean clothing, nothing. So I thought I'd come and save you having to run across the yard. I wouldn't have minded the view, but I didn't mind the view while I was watching you wash, either." Gerry's smile lifted Ghost's heart, and his strong arms closed around Ghost along with the towel.

Ghost gazed up at Gerry's beloved face. "It's mutual, you know. I liked watching you wash the very first morning when the Witch had healed your leg. I was trying not to let you see me, but I was pretty sure you did."

Gerry's laugh was as welcome as his embrace. "I did see you. You're right. You were so shy and skittish, but I couldn't take my eyes off you. Moon shine on me, I was surprised we made it to the table to eat the porridge. I was terrified the Witch was going to do something awful to me too. I hadn't even asked to court you or made my intentions known properly. I just sort of dragged you into bed with me."

"Dragging me was the best way. I'd never have dared let you know I thought you were handsome. Or that you were so brave, coping with the pain as well as you did." Ghost let his head rest against Gerry. "I'd seen other people treated for broken bones, and they screamed like the Witch was breaking the bone all over again. Although once or twice she actually did, when the break had started to set on its own and wasn't right. What a nasty sound, bone breaking."

Ghost sighed. "But I guess we'd better get back in the house. After we eat, I need to blend more herbs for fever and stomach flux, and I want to look in the formulary. I'm so frustrated. I feel like I should have the remedy, but what I'm trying isn't quite right." He twisted around to glance at Gerry. "If I can't figure out what to do by tomorrow night, I'll need to contact the sisterhood to see what they know. I'd rather not deal with them, but I can't simply hope I get the treatment right. This isn't some outbreak of stomach aches from spoiled food. I'm worried that this sickness is a full-blown plague."

"You could try to contact the Witch. You should have a way to send out word you want to speak with her and make it seem like a casual thing." Gerry released Ghost and opened the door to the washhouse. "This way, no one will have any reason to prod at you. But if the malady is a plague, no one should give you any grief."

Ghost walked back to the house, wrapped in the warm towel, his pace brisk. Gerry kept up, one arm still around him.

"Hmm, your idea might be easier," Ghost said. "But if I can't reach the Witch right away, I'll need to ask the sisterhood anyway. In the meanwhile, I've lost time figuring this out. Merrah is all right for now, but four others died today. Three elderly and a newborn. Not Sari's child, thankfully. Another babe not even a quarter moon old. The dam never came to me because the alpha thought she didn't need a healer to bear a babe, even though she was feeling sick. I might have been able to prevent the death if she had." He sighed again. "I wish I could figure this out. There's been no festival in the past quarter moon. For so many to get sick, and with the same symptoms, there has to be a link. I can't see the pattern yet."

"You've just started looking today, and you don't know you could have saved that babe. Don't be so harsh on yourself," Gerry said, following Ghost into the house. He closed the door behind them, waving a hand at Ghost when Ghost started to object. "Go put on clothing. You need food. Afterward, you can leave the door ajar if you want. But if you get sick, you won't be able to help anyone."

Ghost had to admit Gerry was right. Ghost was worried he would be found lacking, and his incompetence would cause the village to demand a proper witch, a woman who would fit the standard image. Ghost could only do so much, though. No witch could do more, and he needed to remember this.

"You're right. I'll get dressed, we'll eat, and then I'll sort out the herbs and check the drying shed for supplies. Tomorrow will bring its own troubles." Ghost felt better for Gerry's support and offered him a wan smile. "Food sounds good. I'll be right out."

Chapter Four

GERRY WATCHED GHOST measuring herbs as he consulted his formulary, glad the meal had given Ghost some color in his cheeks again. Gerry stood and pressed a kiss to Ghost's temple.

"I've got to go. I'm working guard with Mother at the market. I'll ask for a tally stick for ginger root as part of tonight's trade. You can pick the ginger up tomorrow when the market is open." Ghost was absorbed in his mixing and barely nodded his assent. "Try to sleep tonight?"

Ghost glanced up, and Gerry bit back a moan of desire as he looked into those crystalline eyes.

"I'll try. Do you stay until dawn or are you coming home sooner?" Ghost's agile fingers continued to sift the herbs.

"Is this so you know when to sneak into bed so you can pretend to have been there all along?" Gerry teased. "No, I'm joking, beloved. I think we have until high moon. They're splitting the shifts to keep watch on all the goods up from the South. You want to hear the good news? Conn is taking second shift. Another seasoned guard agreed to train him." Gerry nearly laughed at the expression on Ghost's face. "Honestly, it was Conn's idea to train with someone other than Mother. He said Mother was too soft with him, and he wanted to learn the right way. The kid's growing up, and he's turning out to be a good man."

"Conn and I get along fine." Ghost shrugged.

"Now you do," Gerry countered. "He was jealous of you at first, and you weren't any fonder of him. If he hadn't been such a little shit and picked a fight with you, you wouldn't have run off and gotten kidnapped by the ranger in the first place. He had Mother wrapped around his little finger. Conn did nothing but whine, and when he got called on his behavior, he played up to Mother. But that was the first time I saw Mother get sharp with the kid. About time too."

"I'm younger than he is," Ghost said and wrinkled his nose in the way Gerry found far too endearing. "You call him 'kid' like he's not adult already."

"That's because I remember when he was little and Mother first took him in." Gerry grinned. "I need to go, my witch, before Mother comes to drag me off by my ear like I was a kid myself."

Gerry lingered long enough to kiss Ghost. He did not want to leave, but he knew he would get to come home to his mate not only tonight, but every night. Ghost would be waiting for him.

Ghost leaned into Gerry, but Gerry could see the tension he held in his shoulders. Gerry kissed him again. "It'll work out. I'll be home later and we can talk more then." Ghost murmured agreement and returned to mixing.

THE WAREHOUSES WERE packed with goods from the last of the Southron caravans to come in. Crates and barrels overflowed with produce, bolts of well woven fabrics, dried fruits, herbs, and spices, the likes of which could not grow in the Heartlands. Planks of deep-red wood stacked to the ceiling awaited carpenters to turn them into furniture. Towers of barrels held olive oil, sweet-smelling soaps, and tiny dried fish.

The last caravans of the season had left well-laden with trade goods from the Heartlands to take back to the South. Fine furs and well-worked leathers, sturdy barrels filled with mead, dried sind meat, crates of tubers and gourds, and casks of honey all traveled south.

Gerry had spoken to Mother and the merchant, and his share for the night's work was marked on a tally stick so Ghost could exchange the stick for the spices and herbs he wanted. Ginger root was a local commodity, and the merchants had a plentiful stock. Gerry thought back again to the single-minded way Ghost was pursuing this outbreak. Before now, Gerry had never considered the ramifications of living with a healer if a plague broke out.

"You're lost in thought." Mother's deep voice startled him back to the present.

Gerry scrubbed a hand through his hair. "Sorry. Ghost discovered four dead from illness today. He thinks it might be a plague. He's trying to puzzle out what's happening. I'm going to come home to find him still awake and poring over his formulary."

"He's a dedicated witch," Mother said. "The last time I remember an outbreak like this was before you were born. We lost a lot of good people then. Maybe he'll find something in his notes from the Witch."

"I'd rather he not spend all night reading. He's not going to do anyone any good if he's unconscious from exhaustion," Gerry said. "And I can't hand out his herbs and concoctions. I'm no closer to understanding the ancient writing than I was before I met him."

Mother chuckled. "Reading's not as hard as it looks. It takes practice, like any skill."

Gerry looked at Mother in surprise. "You can read?" He had never seen Mother reading anything, other than the pictographs they all used or the tally sticks the merchants offered. Counting and numbering were far more important than reading. Gerry himself could count and use tally sticks just fine. The rest was something he had never even thought about.

"Don't look so surprised," Mother said with a smile. "There's a fair bit about me you don't know. Give me some time to get used to you being a fellow alpha and not my dependent. I need to lose the habit of protecting you. You proved yourself in the ruins when you saved Ghost and Conn."

"I guess I never thought anyone but witches or rangers knew the old writing, and even rangers don't know how to read as well as witches." Gerry shrugged.

Mother's gaze was thoughtful. "My dam was a witch. She taught me the writing." He chuckled as he glanced at Gerry. "I had a dam. I didn't merely spring up out of the soil, you know."

"I know," Gerry said, embarrassed. "I hadn't thought about how or where you'd grown up. Did your dam know the Witch?"

Mother gestured for Gerry to walk with him. "My dam knew the Witch when the Witch was newly come to the sisterhood. The Witch is only eight years older than me. She was supposed to take over for my dam, and so she stayed with us for a time while my dam taught her what was necessary. A good witch knows her village. She keeps track of lessons learned and passes the knowledge on."

They morved into a different room, and the ambrosial smell of spice filled Gerry's nose. Gerry knew how much Ghost would enjoy the rich fragrance filling the air.

"Well, I slipped and let on to the Witch I could read the words. Even then, she could make your blood run cold with a single glance." Mother and Gerry scanned the floors to make sure no scavengers or small animals had gotten in to damage the spices.

Gerry was sure he had to look like a child caught up in a good tale. "What happened?"

Mother chuckled a little. "She asked me what I was going to do with such an unusual skill. The way she said it, well, I can hear her still. Like she was asking me if I was going to take myself in hand in the center of the market and have a good wank."

Mother's comment brought a smile to Gerry's lips. "Now that sounds like her."

AFTER HIS SHIFT, Gerry was not at all surprised to arrive home and see lamps still lit, and a thin trickle of smoke rising from the chimney. Gerry opened the door, and Ghost raised his head, his formulary open and a cup in his hand. Exhaustion had left faint bruises under Ghost's eyes, but he brightened when he saw Gerry.

Ghost stood up and stretched. On the formulary cabinet, Gerry saw a basket full of small linen packets marked with daubs of colored wax. Ghost had been busy, and now he was reading over the ancient text. A scrap of paper was next to the formulary, covered in Ghost's tiny writing.

"Any luck?" Gerry asked.

Ghost frowned and sank back down onto his chair, Gerry sitting across from him. Ghost twisted his white hair with his ink-smudged fingers. From the looks of Ghost's tangled mop, he had been worrying his hair all evening.

"The hunt is frustrating," Ghost admitted. "A dozen references seem to match the symptoms, but then nothing. They just stop short. I'm going to have to contact the sisterhood in the morning."

"You're sure you want to talk to them?" Gerry reached out to capture one restless hand, Ghost's fingers feeling so soft next to his own callused hand. "You're willing to deal with the witches who think you're not supposed to be one of them?"

"I have to face them. I can't hide. Those witches win if I do." He sounded determined, and Gerry felt Ghost's slim fingers tighten. "What's important is finding out what this outbreak is and how to deal with its ravages, before the damned plague gets out of hand. I don't want to be the witch who let his village die because he was scared someone would speak harshly to him. I have to think about the people who are looking to me to help them."

"And what about the Witch herself? Don't you want to try to reach her?" Gerry cupped his free hand around Ghost's cheek. "She might have seen something like this before."

Ghost tangled his fingers with Gerry's. "If she has any information, she'll contact me. But I'm not going to waste time waiting for her. She won't answer a scrying call when she doesn't want to be bothered." He stood, not releasing Gerry's hand. "Let's go to bed. I want to feel you hold me as we go to sleep."

Chapter Five

GHOST SLEPT WELL but woke to an empty bed. He padded to the living room and peeked out the window to find Gerry sitting on the low garden wall, checking over a quiver of arrows. Gerry looked relaxed and thoughtful while enjoying the unusually warm autumn morning, and Ghost wondered what was occupying Gerry's mind. He was unwilling to interrupt, though, turning away quietly.

He decided he had no reasonable excuse to avoid reaching out to the witchsisters. Ghost removed the scrying mirror from the back of his formulary cabinet, unwrapped the soft layers of hide protecting it, and peered into the polished silver surface.

Ghost focused his will as he visualized his message. Unlike many of his other tools, the scrying mirror was not a relic of the ancients. The talent for telepathy marked Ghost as a true witch. Telepathy was the magic that had to be in the blood, the gift of the Seeker herself to her chosen witches. He decided to send an open call to all the sisterhood, although a widespread call was harder and took more out of him. The more witches who heard him, the more likely he was to get responses. His mental voice was strong as he shaped the words around his memories of the patients he had seen.

"Hear me, my sisters. Ghost of the Heartlands seeks your help. An outbreak is attacking my people. I saw the first patients yesterday, and four have died already. They suffer from vomiting and fever. Before they die, blood appears in the vomit and leaks from the mouth and nose. Some of the patients recover, but the old and very young are most susceptible. Does anyone know this disease?"

Several tense minutes passed as Ghost waited for a response. The pressure behind his spiral turned to pain, and Ghost tugged at his hair. Relief filled him when his spiral tingled and the mirror filled with clouds, indicating he had made contact. The shadows on the surface shifted and sorted into the semblance of a deep blue crescent, a witchmark he knew well. The tension left his shoulders in a rush.

"Zereda, my sister," Ghost said, smiling and meaning it. "I'm glad you heard me." Ghost counted the Southron witch as a rare friend among the sisterhood. He took it as a good omen Zereda was the first to answer, even if her reply was not audible. Instead, he heard her voice in his mind, sounding exactly as she would in person.

"Little Ghost brother," Zereda replied, her words slurred and softened by her Southron accent. "You have trouble in your green valley between the mountains. This illness that plagues your people is familiar, and yet not. I will consult my formulary, little brother, and seek answers among the others of our kind here in the South." She paused, her disembodied voice sounding troubled when she resumed. "Be careful in the advice you heed. If you can look within, do so. I feel a strange dread. Curious this happens at a time when the Witch is wandering."

Ghost looked into the mirror, not letting his hold on the conversation waver despite feeling a subtle alarm. "What do you mean?" He waited for Zereda's response.

"The Witch may have stirred things up in places that should not be disturbed, little brother." Zereda still sounded troubled. "This would not be the first time. Though I love her as if she were a true sister, the Witch is ever one to go where she should not and to seek out what should be left hidden. I do not know if the Seeker guides her steps or the Seeker's dread mate. You may be able to *see* the Witch more clearly than I would in this instance. But all I have *seen* tells me the Witch may have the answers you seek."

The notion of dealing with the hidden Eighth was enough to coax a shudder from Ghost. "Your advice isn't making me want to try to *see* the Witch, you know. And you've been a seer far longer than I have. I'd have thought you'd be better able to track her."

"You have not even tried," Zereda chided. "She has cloaked such knowledge from my Sight."

Ghost shook his head in dismay, even though Zereda could not see him. "I haven't felt her, but I haven't tried either."

"You *saw* something the other night. I felt you in the wake of the Seeker's passing. Did the vision not help? Or was your *seeing* for another purpose?" Zereda's witchmark sharpened until Ghost could almost make out her eyes in the mirror, or perhaps he was *seeing* them. They were narrowed, whether in concentration or in concern, he could not tell.

"What I *saw* may be connected. I don't know for sure. I need to think. I get very frustrating riddles." Ghost sighed and felt the ripple of amusement from the Southron witch.

"Do you think the Seeker makes her messages easy for any of us who are given this gift? The gods never speak plain. You should know this, little brother." Zereda relented after a moment. "The riddles have a pattern to them. You must turn them over in your mind and see them as the gods would. They are not hampered by our small concerns, our need for food and shelter and companionship. I do not even think they require our love and worship. I would offer both still, and freely, for they are worthy of my worship. But never expect them to speak plain."

Ghost pondered the words of the Southron witch. "I'll keep this in mind, my sister. If I think the vision is linked to either the illness or to the Witch, I'll contact you. I promise." He could sense the smile in Zereda's mental voice.

"The Witch always said your promise was a thing of value. You do not offer promises lightly, and you do not break oaths. I will accept your promise, and thank you for the trust. Now go, little brother. Do what a Ghost does best and look between the known and the unknown," Zereda said. "And I shall look in my formulary and ask my questions about this outbreak of yours." She broke off as a new mind joined the conversation.

"Ghost, brother." A new sending appeared in the mirror, an amber flame joining the blue crescent. Kerree's mental voice was brighter than Zereda's voice, her accent lilting.

"Kerree, thank you, sister," Ghost said, welcoming the witch from the East Marches. The Witch had told Ghost the East Marches were more a chain of islands than an actual landmass. Many from the East preferred to live on their swift ships, never setting foot on soil if they could help it. Landbound in the high valley of the Heartlands, the East had seemed a wondrous place to Ghost when he was small. Perhaps he had a touch of the Witch's own wanderlust. But that was a thought for another time, and he dragged his mind back to the conversation. "Do you have any knowledge of this plague?"

"Your outbreak sounds more like one of the legendary engineered illnesses, rather than a natural disease." Kerree sounded entirely certain. "We've seen such things before. You take a virus from this and some bacteria from thus, and you make a new contagion, like blending extracts to make a serum. The few relics we have are not the only ones that survived from the ancient cities. Stories abound of spinning devices used to combine phages and bacteria."

"And such things are best not discussed on an open sending." Zereda's words took on a stern edge in Ghost's mind.

"It's not a mystery, Zereda. Unless you've *seen* otherwise. I want to help our little brother." Kerree waited a beat and then resumed. "Like you, I keep thinking I should know this one. It's on the tip of my fingers, almost. I'll dig in my notes as well, and see what I can find, and I'll pester the godsman here for records as well. They like their notes, the godsmen do."

The mirror flickered and Ghost registered a surge of contempt as a red dagger gleamed for an instant and vanished.

"Oh, lovely," Kerree growled. "Sri popped in, didn't she? Wester hag."

Zereda's mental snort was eloquent.

Ghost sighed. Sri of the West Reaches was one of the louder voices declaring him an abomination. He knew she had let herself show merely to keep him on edge and give those witches who would speak with him pause for thought. Before he could speak, the mirror flickered again. A green leaf formed, the color brighter than his olivine spiral.

Kerree growled again. "Figures you'd chime in, Beccah. You barely missed Sri. Did she let you out for the night?"

Beccah's voice was as musical as Kerree's voice, the East Marches her home as well. "I'm a lot of things, sweet sister, but I'm a witch first. I may not like having a male witch, but a plague comes before my likes. And as far as Sri goes, well, I'm not so certain you're off the mark when you mention created disease vectors. But we should talk face-to-face, and you know where I anchor." Her mental voice sharpened. "As to you, Ghost, be wary. I'll look through my notes. If I find anything at all that can help you, I'll share what I learn. We're not all blind to our primary responsibility as healers."

"I'd be grateful, Beccah." Ghost shrugged off a nagging sense of unease and returned to the conversation. "Thank you all for your help. Until I hear from you, I'll do the best I can. My mate's traded a night's work for more herbs, and I'll make good use of them, I'm afraid."

"Did you make it official?" Kerree sounded delighted. "Joy to you, Ghost. May the Moon shine on you both. Now, let me go check my notes and prod the godsman. I'll send to you if I find anything." The amber flame disappeared.

"I also must go, my brother. Be well, and do as I have said, little Ghost. Answers exist even when we cannot puzzle out the meanings. Clarity will come." Zereda's crescent faded, and Ghost looked at the mirror, with its green leaf still showing.

"Before I leave you, Ghost of the Heartlands, let me say this. I have no cause to love you, but if the Seeker has chosen you, I'd be a fool to oppose her. A word of advice. Seek out Tal of the West Reaches. Her mark is knotwork in crimson." Beccah's green leaf faded, and the mirror was merely a polished piece of silver once more.

Ghost's head ached, and the stones of his spiral felt hot and raw. He stood up with care, his whole body tender. He wrapped the scrying mirror in its runner hide and returned the bundle to the drawer of his formulary cabinet.

Ghost did not want Gerry to see him like this, and so he reached up for one of the pottery jars. He took a few of the leaves, put the jar away, and went to the kitchen to make a tisane. It was not often he resorted to so potent a remedy, but the scrying had been difficult. If Zereda was right, he would need to open himself to *see* later tonight, and starting with an aching head was not wise.

Kerree had ventured the possibility this illness was artificial. Ghost remembered something from the Witch's notes about engineered illnesses. Now, more than ever, he needed to talk to the Witch. He would have to use his Sight to find a clever witch who did not want to be found.

But first, Ghost wanted to relieve the throbbing in his head. The tisane would help there. He had patients to see in the village this afternoon, and a clear head was essential. And if the Seeker smiled on him, he would have answers tonight.

Chapter Six

GHOST TUGGED AT Gerry's tunic as Gerry washed the dinner dishes. "What are you doing?" Gerry turned from his task to raise his eyebrow at Ghost.

"Leave the dishes. I'll wash them later, when you've gone. Come and sit with me," Ghost pleaded.

Ghost had spent the afternoon visiting his patients in the village. Two of them, both elderly men, were not getting any stronger. Still, no one else had died. Ghost would take what small victories he could get.

The light of the room made the hint of brown in Gerry's eyes flicker as Ghost gazed up into them. "I've finished seeing patients for the day. The packets are all ready for tomorrow's visits, thanks to you and your tally stick. And I have to wait to hear back from the sisterhood. So let's sit and relax until you have to go."

"We don't just sit and relax," Gerry teased as he followed Ghost to the main room. Ghost settled into Gerry's arms on the padded, high-backed bench in front of the smaller hearth.

"Well, what do we do?" Ghost asked. Gerry had the faintest shadow of stubble along his jaw. Ghost ran a finger over the bristly whiskers to feel the enticing roughness. "If we don't just sit, of course."

Gerry stroked Ghost's hair. "We do this. You touch and tease. Sooner or later, I lean over and kiss you. Clothing hits the floor, and we hope we remembered to close the front door."

Ghost laughed and brushed a kiss over Gerry's lips. "I didn't think I was teasing. I'm only teasing if we don't wind up with clothes all over and me making all those noises. I'll have you know, I never squeaked before I met you." He slipped his hands into Gerry's thick hair, the brown giving way to deep russet where the sun had lightened the strands.

"You do more than squeak. You purr like a sind's whelp. You yowl a little too, at exactly the right moments." Gerry caught Ghost's mouth in a deeper kiss. Gerry's breath was warm against Ghost's cheek as he spoke. "You blush and you growl. I want to keep you like you are right then. All smooth, bare skin and pink cheeks. Your eyes shining up at me brighter than your witchmark."

Ghost could feel his cheeks heating, ignited by Gerry's description. The words were said with such love, a love Ghost returned without reservation. Ghost opened his mouth to reply, but all that emerged was a faint moan.

"See? Exactly like this," Gerry said with a laugh, and he kissed Ghost again. Ghost succumbed to the growing heat of Gerry's kiss. When he finally released Ghost's mouth, Ghost was dizzy with desire. "Now how am I supposed to sit and relax when you're so kissable?"

Ghost did not get a chance to answer, and his hand tightened in Gerry's hair as Gerry kissed him again. He moved closer, pressing against Gerry. His belly fluttered with the excitement of having Gerry next to him like this.

By the time they broke the kiss, Ghost was quite sorry Gerry needed to work. He knew he needed to prepare himself to *see* later, but Gerry was here now, and he was reluctant to let Gerry leave. Ghost rubbed his cheek against the light stubble on Gerry's jaw and sighed.

"I should let you go," Ghost murmured. "Are you hunting tomorrow?"

"No," Gerry replied, his lips brushing Ghost's temple.

Ghost smiled. "Wake me when you get home. I'll be the naked one in the bed."

Gerry growled, and Ghost laughed at the expression on his face. Gerry's heated look clearly meant he would be sure to wake Ghost. Exactly what Ghost wanted.

GHOST FINISHED CLEANING up the kitchen after Gerry left, as he had said he would do. Once he was done, he reached into the very back of his formulary cabinet and pulled out a worn canvas sack. Ghost handled the small pouch as though the contents were precious beyond measure, and to a witch, they were. He took the sack to the main room and curled up on the floor in front of the smaller hearth.

When Ghost opened the bag, the aroma of pungent herbs wafted up to his nose. He breathed in the scent and felt a tingle of warmth behind his spiral. Beneath the linen wrapper holding the herbs were a shallow silver bowl, a small vial, and a slender blade of obsidian, chipped by his own hand to a razor edge. The grip of the blade was wrapped in thin strips of pure-white hide, given to him by the Witch. Ghost placed the silver bowl in front of the hearth and laid the blade on the bowl's edge.

Ghost stood and stripped off his clothing, folding the garments and leaving them on the padded bench. He pulled the tie from his hair, letting his mane fall loose around his shoulders and down his back. He knelt in front of the silver bowl, removed one of the tiny bundles of twigs and dried leaves from the linen wrapper, and placed it in the center of the shallow bowl. He added a drop of potent sind musk from the vial and grasped the obsidian blade in his right hand.

Ghost took several deep breaths, slow and even, reaching into himself to find the magic that marked him as a true seer. Scrying required him to look outward. Forcing a vision was about *seeing* within and required perfect balance between the waking and dreaming worlds. Tonight he would be alone and vulnerable, but he had to lower his mental shields far enough to permit the vision. He could not afford to be afraid.

"Seeker, guide me." His voice was firm and even as he recited the simple rhyme that served as a trigger for his subconscious mind. "Let me *see* beneath the shadows. Let me *see* beneath the skin. Let me *see* beneath the mystery. Let me *see* what lies within." He raised his hands, and the small bundle in the bowl ignited.

Ghost inhaled the acrid, white smoke that rose from the bowl and enveloped him. He winced as his spiral flared to painful life, hot against his brow. The vivid green light from his witchmark tinted the thick smoke surrounding him. He felt no pain when the cool black edge of the obsidian blade opened his left palm, and the drops of blood sizzled as they fell into the dish.

"Seeker, guide me. Let the End avert his eyes and *see* me not." Ghost finished the prayer, his voice still strong and clear, despite the thick smoke. He inhaled once more and held the smoke in his lungs. The obsidian blade slipped out of his hand as he crumpled to the floor, and the vision overtook him.

GHOST'S ENTIRE BODY ached when he woke. He was cold, and the small hearth was dark and empty. His left hand throbbed, while his mouth tasted of ashes. His stomach lurched at the smell of the sticky residue in the shallow bowl.

"Never easy," Ghost croaked to the empty room, his words sounding hollow against the silence. He pulled himself up to a sitting position, and his head spun. The remnants of the vision floated all around him. He stood, careful not to grab the bench with his left hand.

"First things first." Ghost picked up the soiled bowl and the obsidian knife and took them to the kitchen to be washed. He rinsed off his left hand to look at the palm.

Ghost took it as a good omen that the wound was shallow. The blood had been accepted, and the dreaded Eighth had looked away. He washed away the clotted blood, letting the thin line bleed freely for a moment before he rinsed the cut again with clean water. Ghost could not afford a wound, not when he still had no answers about the outbreak manifesting in the village. The gods' light closed the small gash quickly, only the faintest pink line showing when he was done.

Ghost returned the cleaned bowl and blade to the canvas sack and placed the bundle back into the drawer, behind a jumble of other oddments. The powerful hallucinogens in his smoke bundles were not meant for Gerry, or anyone else. Ghost drew a cup of cool water to help clear the lingering taste of ashes from his tongue and relit the fire in the smaller hearth. Still naked, Ghost padded into the bedroom, sitting back against the headboard to sip his water and reflect on what he had *seen*.

The Witch was indeed cloaking herself, but a bond had been forged between them when she placed a spiral of peridot on the forehead of a frightened little boy plagued by dreams and visions he could not explain. The bond allowed Ghost to find the Witch, and while he had not *seen* her exact location, he had *seen* enough. She had hinted more than once before she left that she was going north, and the vision said she had told the truth.

The vision had shown the Witch, bundled in a cloak of fur as white as the snow circling around her. Her gray hair appeared far more silvery than when she had dwelled in the Heartlands. Her eyes were as dark as ever and stood out in the unrelenting whiteness of the landscape. She had been confident and unafraid in the vision. Of course, the Witch always projected an air of unassailable calm, but her confidence in the vision felt genuine to Ghost.

The Witch would be of little help, though. She had shielded her mind from all telepathic contact, and even their bond would not let Ghost break through to her. Travel to and from the Northlands was hard at best, and with winter approaching, she would find it near impossible to return before the thaw, even if she had heard him. Ghost had hoped to have the Witch beside him, but he needed to accept he was on his own with this outbreak. He would have only what he could glean from the sisterhood and his own progress in treating this illness. He would likely lose more lives before this was done, a prospect Ghost did not relish.

Ghost sipped his water, letting the cool liquid soothe the last of the smoke-induced soreness from his throat. In the morning, he would try to figure out any pattern in the way the plague was spreading. In the back of his mind, the warning from Kerree loomed. If this was not chance, any misstep could prove deadly. Ghost did his best to push aside his growing dread until exhaustion finally won and he succumbed to a fitful sleep.

GERRY ADMIRED GHOST'S peaceful form as he slept. The last of the moonlight cast the angles of Ghost's face into sharp relief. His snowy hair spilled over the pillow in a fall of gilded silver. Ghost's bare arm rested above his head and his hand was open. His agile fingers were still for a change.

As the weather grew colder, Ghost had given up sleeping naked and had taken to wearing one of the far-too-large knitted tunics he had brought with him from the Witch's house. He had whispered to Gerry one night how the Witch had made them with her own hands, and although she could never get the size right, the garments made Ghost feel safe. But the bare arm was an indication Ghost had forgone warmth and comfort tonight in favor of this tempting invitation.

Gerry left his boots by the door and moved silently into the bedroom. He undressed in no time at all and slipped under the quilt. He reached for Ghost's warm, lithe body. Ghost smiled and turned to him, mumbling indistinctly as Gerry pulled Ghost close. Gerry's cock stiffened as Ghost pressed against him, and he was not at all surprised to feel Ghost respond in the same way.

"You're home," Ghost murmured. He nuzzled up against Gerry's jaw. "I'm naked."

"I can tell," Gerry replied before he captured Ghost's mouth in a kiss. Ghost tasted sweet, like honey and Southron apricots, and Gerry deepened the kiss. Ghost's pale eyes opened gradually, and his fingers burrowed in Gerry's hair.

"I missed you," Gerry murmured into the kiss. He gazed at his beloved Ghost and registered the urgency in the way Ghost pressed against him, triggering a pang of alarm. "What's wrong?"

"Later," Ghost murmured. He draped one leg over Gerry's thigh, his cock brushing against Gerry. "I missed you too."

Gerry tried to decipher Ghost's mood for a moment longer and sighed. Whatever was troubling him, Ghost was more interested in making love, and Gerry was not about to argue. At least, his cock was not about to argue.

"Whatever you say, beloved," Gerry replied. He covered Ghost's eager mouth in another kiss. Gerry glided his hands up Ghost's lean torso until his fingers fit into the grooves of Ghost's ribs. He skated one thumb over a pink nipple and earned a squeak.

Ghost's cheeks were already flushed as pink as his nipples. He gasped as Gerry tweaked one tight nub. Ghost's cock jumped, smearing precome as the head brushed against Gerry's belly.

"What's your pleasure tonight?" Gerry murmured. He watched Ghost's eyes widen a fraction. "I'm going to make love to you, but how do you want me?"

Ghost offered up a breathless laugh and wriggled free of Gerry. He scrabbled around for the bottle on the bedside table before handing the oil to Gerry with a wicked smile. He turned and crouched on his knees and elbows, presenting his rounded cheeks. Ghost glanced over his shoulder, and Gerry was struck again at how well he managed both innocence and wanton welcome at the same moment.

"I'd like you to take me like this," Ghost said, his tone a husky drawl. His voice sent a shiver down Gerry's spine, as clear a signal of desire as Ghost's promise to wait in their bed naked. A promise he had fulfilled.

A noise somewhere between a moan and a growl escaped Gerry. He opened the oil and dribbled a generous amount on his fingers. He coated Ghost's tight entrance, and he could feel Ghost's hole quivering as he stroked, the muscle responding to his touch. Ghost pressed back just enough, and Gerry let one finger breach his precious Ghost. Gerry's reward was a mewl as Ghost bowed his back and raised his buttocks, dropping his chest closer to the bed.

"Oh, like this," Ghost whispered. He turned his head to peer at Gerry, eyes smoldering with lust. "Exactly like this."

For once, Ghost did not beg Gerry to hurry or insist he could not wait while Gerry prepared him. He watched Gerry with those shimmering eyes, darker now in the dimness of the room, but he held his position. Gerry marveled at Ghost's restraint but attributed it to Ghost's concern over the village. Ghost needed to forget his fears for this little while.

Ghost's breath hitched when Gerry hooked his fingers, rubbing the spot that made Ghost's purr escalate to a yowl. Gerry's balls drew up in response, and he could not wait a moment longer. He dribbled a little more oil on his fingers and coated his cock well, his precome mixing with the oil.

"My precious Ghost," Gerry whispered. His fingers gripped Ghost's alabaster cheeks, thumbs delving deep to spread the hole.

"Yes, please," Ghost begged.

Gerry's cock jumped at the pure need in the husky plea. Gerry nudged forward, slowly and deliberately, and growled as the head of his cock sank in past Ghost's outer ring. Ghost pushed back with a whimper of lusty desire. Ghost's thighs trembled as Gerry eased in farther. Gerry paused, as he always did, wanting to give Ghost a chance to adjust to the intrusion. Ghost huffed a breath and all but growled.

"Feels so good. I'm ready, Gerry. Move for me. I want to feel you move in me."

Gerry eased in a little more with short, gentle thrusts and heard Ghost hiss in pleasure. He wrapped his arm around Ghost's chest and sat back on his heels, pulling Ghost with him. He settled Ghost onto his thighs. Gerry's hands skated down to wrap around Ghost's hips.

"What are you—" Ghost's question broke off in a moan as Gerry rocked him a fraction, and Gerry's cock moved inside him.

"You like this?" Gerry whispered. Ghost's hair tickled Gerry's chest as Ghost nodded. "It's even better like this. You'll see."

Gerry guided Ghost up with firm hands around his hips and lifted Ghost off his cock until only the head remained inside. Gerry lowered Ghost, and Ghost let out a soft cry signaling Gerry's cock had hit the precise spot he had sought.

Gerry continued to guide Ghost until they found an easy rhythm. Gerry reached around to wrap one hand around Ghost's cock. Ghost's slick precome dribbled down the shaft from the dusky head. Gerry stroked Ghost's cock and slid his thumb over the slit. He glanced over Ghost's shoulder and saw the precome he had smeared glistening in the faint moonlight coming through the window. Lover's light, he told himself and smiled into the tangle of Ghost's hair.

Ghost rose and fell on Gerry's cock, his movements almost languid as Gerry guided him, a faint sheen of sweat on Ghost's thighs. Gerry drifted one hand up Ghost's chest to find a pebbled nipple. He tweaked the tender nub and coaxed another cry from Ghost. Ghost's cock jumped as Gerry stroked it, and Gerry knew Ghost was close to release.

"Ghost. Let go for me," Gerry urged. Ghost's spine arched and his head fell back. His glossy hair brushed against Gerry's shoulder and neck.

Ghost's voice was raspy as he begged, "Please, just a little more." Ghost lifted himself and came down sharply. Ghost yelped and the already tight passage clenched even more around Gerry's cock. Ghost's cock twitched in Gerry's hand, and hot come spilled over Gerry's fingers. Ghost ground down on Gerry's cock with a sob of pleasure.

Gerry could not hold back any longer. His balls tightened, and the heat in his belly spread through him like wildfire. Gerry registered Ghost grinding down on him, and white light filled his vision as he came.

"Gods, Ghost." Gerry groaned. He tightened his arms around Ghost, shuddering as Ghost went limp against him. Ghost's breath was ragged. He buried his face in Ghost's soft hair, inhaling his unique scent and trying to control his own harsh panting. A few long moments passed before he realized Ghost was sobbing.

"Hey, what's this?" Gerry held Ghost tighter, one hand coaxing Ghost to turn and look at him. "Did I hurt you? Are you all right?"

Ghost shook his head and took a deep breath. "It's not you. You've never hurt me." He hiccupped. "I tried to *see* the Witch tonight while you were out. I guess I was feeling a little raw."

Gerry eased Ghost off his cock and turned Ghost around. Ghost straddled Gerry and crossed his ankles behind Gerry's back. Gerry looked at the witch, intent. "You forced a vision? I didn't even know you could do such a thing." Gerry's fingers were gentle as he wiped away the tears from Ghost's cheeks.

"I'm able to push the Sight when I'm healing someone, but forcing a vision requires you to open yourself up. Wide open. Scary to feel vulnerable." Ghost sniffled and offered a weak smile. "I'm not as fierce as the Witch, I know. I do have ways to defend myself. After the ranger, I made the Witch teach me. But this is different because you have to let down your shields and allow whatever else can *see* you have a chance at you."

"Gods, Ghost," Gerry said again, gentler this time. "Did you have to be alone? Because I would have been here for you, if I could. I don't ever want you to feel like you're in danger or on your own. I'm your mate and your alpha. My job is to protect you."

"Like with the ranger." Ghost's smile was stronger. "I knew you'd find me. I knew you'd come. And even though I was scared, I didn't lose hope." Ghost wrapped his arms around Gerry and squeezed him tight. "I don't know for sure if you can be there when I force a vision. I have to ask. I know one witchsister who's also a seer. But I burn certain herbs to help me let go of the waking world, and I don't know if they'd hurt you."

Gerry risked a small chuckle. Ghost rested his head against Gerry's shoulder and Gerry pressed a kiss to his sweat-dampened hair.

"I'm supposed to be the alpha, you know," Gerry teased, and he was glad to hear the little snort from Ghost.

"And I'm a witch. We take care of people too. And for the most part, we're not supposed to place people in danger." Ghost's voice had steadied. "I guess we're two of a kind, aren't we? I don't think we should let the godsman know."

It was a weak joke, but Gerry was grateful for the feeble humor. He did his best to keep his own voice light. "Oh, I don't know. We could start a whole new custom." He smirked when Ghost gave him a quizzical glance. "Mother says most witches are alphas, when you come down to it."

Ghost snorted. "Between what Mother says and what the Witch used to say, we don't even have to think. Our former alphas are thinking for us." Ghost tilted his head for a kiss. "Let's sleep a while. I have to go to the village, but I can sleep a while longer."

"Aren't you going to tell me how the vision went? Did you find the Witch?" Gerry let Ghost wriggle free and settle down among the pillows. He pulled the quilt up over them both as he lay down beside Ghost.

Ghost frowned and shook his head. "I *saw* her, but nothing was clear. If I'm right, she's in the Northlands, which means I'm on my own. I can't wait for her to get here." Ghost turned on his side and burrowed closer to Gerry. "I have to believe I'll find a solution. I can't talk myself into failing. So, I'm going to sleep and go to the village in the morning and figure this out." He closed his eyes, a clear signal he desired to end the discussion.

Gerry smiled at the return of his fierce witch. "Sounds like a good plan." He nuzzled Ghost's hair and hummed an old lullaby until Ghost's breathing evened out.

Chapter Seven

THE MYSTERIOUS CONTAGION was ravaging the village. Ghost ran a hand through his hair, his fingers catching in a tangle, and he pulled them free with a weary sigh. In a mere quarter moon, one street had become more than a hand of streets, with no pattern Ghost could discern. More patients had died, and Ghost knew they would not be the last. If the deceased had no family, the guards who worked the warehouses took the bodies for burial.

Ghost stretched to ease the tightness in his back as he walked home from the last house needing help on this street. High sun was well past. All Ghost could do was offer the infusion of herbs to ease the purging and lower the fever. In the worst cases, where the patient had begun to hemorrhage, the Seeker's kiss brought some relief from the aches from prolonged vomiting. But with a growing number of sick villagers, Ghost needed to conserve the relic to ensure it lasted the day before needing to be fed.

Ghost stumbled over a loose stone in front of a small house, and as he caught himself, he heard a feeble cry. He stared for a moment at the door, unable to recall if he had ever visited this house. Set back as the building was from the street, the house was nearly hidden from view. Another cry galvanized him, and he hurried inside.

He found an old man in the kitchen. How he had not fallen was beyond Ghost's comprehension. Dried blood covered the front of his tunic, and fresh trails of crimson spattered his beard. The man clutched a wet cloth.

"She wants me to help her wash," the man said, his voice weak and ragged.

Ghost took the cloth and placed his arm around the man's waist. "Show me. I'll help you." He let the man guide him into the small bedroom.

A woman huddled in the bed, so still Ghost feared she had already died. Her eyes opened, and Ghost could see the blood in them where small vessels had ruptured from the force of her vomiting. She lacked strength enough to turn her head, but her eyes softened when she looked at the old man.

"She got sick. I did what I could until I got sick too." The old man shrugged off Ghost's arm and sat on the bed. "We both know there's no hope. I just don't want to leave her alone."

Ghost swallowed hard and looked for words. "I'm a healer, but when I can't heal... When you feel his approach, I can ease the way. I have a tincture, the Seeker's rest that will bring a painless death. You'll fall asleep. I can offer the tincture, but you have to choose to accept its respite."

"Will we die together?" The old man took the woman's fragile hand, stroking the wrinkled skin as he watched Ghost.

"Yes." Ghost waited while the old man turned to the woman.

"What do you say, sweetheart? One last walk together?" The man's smile was gentle. The woman's fingers twitched, and the man turned back to Ghost. "Please. Help us die. We're ready. We're not afraid."

"Come then." Ghost helped the man settle next to the woman, her eyes never leaving the man. He left them long enough to get two cups of water, adding three drops of the tincture to each cup. As weak as they were, he did not need more. "This is a little bitter, but you won't hurt any longer. I promise you, on my vows as a witch. You'll have a peaceful death."

The man took one cup, and Ghost helped the woman to drink from the other. She grimaced, but she swallowed all of the tincture, her hand still resting in the old man's hand. She closed her eyes and sighed. The man let Ghost take his empty cup, and Ghost saw the lines of pain soften before the man closed his eyes.

Ghost waited, watching as their breathing slowed and finally stopped. He used the wet cloth to clean them both as best as he could, rinsing the cloth in a bucket of cool water. He scrubbed his hands and left the house, stopping to ask a guard to take the couple for burial before he continued on his way home. His eyes burned with exhaustion and tears. Each death was a blow, and he wondered if he would ever get used to watching a patient die, or if he would always feel so bereaved.

Ghost had left clean clothing and a towel in the washhouse. When he reached the yard, he made straight for the back. He tossed a couple of knots of hardwood on the fire beside the deep copper tub, watching the steam rise from the water.

A persistent tightness burrowed between Ghost's shoulder blades, and his eyes felt gritty. He scrubbed, rinsed off, and scrubbed a second time. Only then did he dry himself and dress. He was stiff, and the tightness between his shoulders had not eased, but he could almost be sure he would not carry the illness into his home. He stopped at the drying shed and left his Seeker's kiss to be fed by the witchglass. That done, he rummaged among the bundles for more of the herbs he needed.

Gerry was not home, and Ghost remembered Gerry had planned to investigate a possible sind lair too close to a farm with some of the other hunters. He went to his formulary cabinet and pulled out the scrying mirror, unwrapping the smooth piece of metal in the hopes he would be contacted. While he waited, there were herbs to blend.

The rote work left Ghost free to think about the *seeing* he had forced. Ghost had *seen* stones carved with witchmarks in a landscape filled with swirling white and gleaming ice. He had *seen* the Witch in the snow as well, in a cloak made of pure white fur. He found it impossible not to conclude the Witch was in the Northlands, but why? Ghost could not fathom what she would want to find in the fabled wilderness beyond the mountains.

A sharp tug on his spiral turned Ghost's attention to the mirror, and he had to look twice at the symbol forming in the white swirl. A ruby triskele filled the mirror, and the familiar dry voice of the Witch echoed in his mind.

"Ah, there you are, little one. Has it started?" The Witch sounded impatient, and Ghost took a sharp breath.

"Has what started?" he asked. He willed the image in the mirror to clear, but the swirl of white stubbornly refused to resolve into anything meaningful.

The Witch's mental snort was like having her there beside Ghost. "The epidemic. Has the epidemic started?"

"The sisterhood reached you, then. Did Zereda find you? She was the first I spoke to." Ghost frowned at the mirror. "Kerree says this isn't natural."

"Kerree's no fool. I don't have a lot of time, little one. Listen to me carefully." The Witch's voice dropped, as if she was afraid even this magical link would be overheard. "The problem started in the South, but the answer is here in the Northlands."

"I'd have guessed the West Reaches with Sri and her ilk, but I don't like Sri, so I'm inclined to blame her," Ghost said, his voice nearly as soft. Whatever had the Witch apprehensive made Ghost wary as well.

Ghost heard the snort again. "I tell him to listen, and so he talks. While I'm glad you've finally found your tongue, this is not the time. I may have the solution, but the trick is going to be getting out of here. I'm going to try—"

The Witch's mental voice broke off abruptly, and Ghost's mirror cleared as though the other mirror had been covered in haste. He winced with the sudden withdrawal, and his spiral felt hot and itchy.

GHOST LEFT HIS mirror uncovered as he walked over to the hearth and moved the kettle closer to the heat. The front door was propped open, and as Ghost looked up, he saw Gerry coming down the path.

"You look exhausted," Gerry said as Ghost opened the door the rest of the way for him.

"I'm fine," Ghost replied. "I'm making an infusion for my headache. The plague is spreading rapidly, and I have far too many new cases. At least three hands' worth who have me worried."

Ghost sighed as Gerry wrapped his arms around Ghost and kissed his forehead.

"Go sit down. I'll make tea. You have a headache because you didn't eat." Gerry reached for the teapot. "Cut some bread for us both. Do you want the nut butter?"

Ghost blinked at Gerry. "I don't really have time to eat. I need to see the elders to ask for an empty warehouse to isolate the infected. I also need to get in touch with one of the witchsisters."

"And this is exactly why you need to stop and eat." Gerry set the spread on the table. "I'll go with you to see the elders. I can add my voice as your alpha. Not as though you need me, since you're speaking as our witch. But you won't be able to help anyone if you let yourself get exhausted and rundown."

Ghost's stomach grumbled. "All right, maybe a piece of bread," he conceded. "I heard from the Witch too. She was sort of cryptic."

"Where is she? Did she say?" Gerry poured tea for them both.

Ghost added a small bit of honey to his tea. He took a slice of the bread and smeared some nut butter over it, licking a stray bit from his finger.

"She's in the Northlands. She asked if the epidemic had started yet," Ghost said. "She said something about maybe having a solution, but she cut off contact without warning. I'm hoping she contacts me again, or one of the other witches does. I can't lose any more patients, even though I know I will."

Gerry winced, reaching out to take Ghost's hand. "You lost people today? I'm sorry, Ghost."

"Seven so far. And another three who probably won't make the next quarter moon." Ghost sighed and rubbed his eyes. "The worst part? The old and the very young are the most vulnerable. Everyone else seems to recover without too much trouble. But the ones who need me the most are dying, and I hate being so impotent."

Gerry looked troubled, and his thumb rubbed Ghost's palm. "The alpha in me needs to keep others safe. This, though. There's nothing I can do. I can't imagine how hard this is for you."

"The Witch said something about trouble getting the solution out, but she was cut off." Ghost opened his mouth to speak and then closed it again.

"What? Tell me, Ghost." Gerry let go of Ghost's hand in favor of lifting Ghost's chin.

"The witches I spoke to earlier? One of them hinted this was not a natural illness. The Witch seemed to agree, and her agreement scares me." Ghost looked at Gerry, not trying to hide how troubled he was. "If someone wanted this outbreak to happen, what if they found the Witch?"

Gerry looked dubious. "How would they go about finding her? I thought seers were rare. If she didn't tell you, I doubt she'd have told anyone where she was headed."

"Seers *are* rare. The only other one I know of is Zereda. She's a friend of the Witch from way back, and she helped me when I started having visions." Ghost frowned. "She said she was blocked from *seeing* where the Witch was. I managed it because I was the Witch's apprentice. We share a bond because the Witch gave me my witchmark."

"Then the Witch is probably fine. She can take care of herself." Gerry did not sound very convinced, though, and Ghost shook his head.

"I know she can take care of herself, but you can't always protect yourself from every danger." Ghost ran his hand through his hair, wondering how to explain to Gerry. "She's in the Northlands. I have no idea how they treat witches, or if they even understand what we are. I don't know if they have ruins or use relics. They're a mystery, and on top of an inexplicable illness, I don't trust another mystery. Then there's the way the contact was cut off, like she'd covered the mirror to hide it from someone. Or like someone had taken the mirror from her."

Gerry looked at the table for a moment, staring a hole through his bread, and Ghost knew he was thinking hard. Gerry's fingers tapped a staccato rhythm on the table. When Gerry looked up, his expression was somber.

"What do you want to do?" Gerry asked.

Ghost was sure his own surprise was written all over his face. "What do you mean? You're my alpha. I should be asking you, or at least asking your leave to do whatever it is I want to do."

Gerry shook his head in negation. "Not this time. This is witch's business, and I don't claim any right to decide for you about this. I don't really care what the godsman said at our mating ceremony, or how the elders would feel about it. There are going to be times when I have to step aside as your alpha and let you choose your path. You're a witch, and I can't know what needs doing."

Ghost had not expected Gerry's answer, and he took a deep breath. "And if I ask you for advice?"

"I'll give it without hesitation." Gerry gave Ghost's hand a gentle squeeze. "But my usefulness might be limited since I don't think I know enough about the problem."

Ghost's thoughts were a jumble as he considered his options. Gerry's trust in his wisdom was heartening, but Ghost was far less confident he would choose the correct path to follow.

"I need to talk to the witchsisters again, and I can only hope the Witch contacts me with the rest of what she wanted to say. I'll admit I'm worried about her. The way the contact ended was too abrupt, and not like her at all." Ghost picked up the last bit of his bread and ate it, chewing as he thought. "Would you stop me if I said I wanted to go north?"

"I'd ask to go with you," Gerry said. His mud-green eyes never wavered as he looked at Ghost. The love and trust he offered without hesitation rocked Ghost to his core.

"If I said I had to go alone?" Ghost hated himself for persisting, but he needed to know. Gerry's answer would affect his decision, and he would be foolish to pretend otherwise.

Gerry sighed. "Then I'd have to let you go, or I'd have been lying when I said I trusted you to know what needs doing as our healer. You're this village's witch, even if you're my Ghost. I can't hold you back from what you need to do."

"I'm sorry," Ghost said, and he meant the apology. "I don't know if I'll need to go. I won't know until I talk to my sisters. And with this plague running through the village, I don't really want to leave. My first duty is to my village. Duty is part of taking the oath as a witch. I passed their tests and I took their oath. I need to honor my vows. Otherwise, I'm not worth much at all, am I?"

Ghost drank the last of the tea and realized he did feel better for having eaten. He stood and stretched.

"For now, I need to talk to the elders about getting a warehouse to isolate and treat the sick." Ghost regarded Gerry with a small smile. "Did you mean it about lending your voice to mine as my alpha?"

Gerry stood and held out his hand to Ghost. "Of course I did. I think they'll have to listen to the both of us, don't you?"

GHOST AND GERRY walked in silence to the chamber of the elders, next to the gods' house. Ghost was busy rehearsing his request in his mind, hoping the words did not get tangled on his tongue. The warmth of Gerry's hand was welcome when Ghost reached for him.

The door from the antechamber to where the elders waited was open. Ghost and Gerry entered, Ghost peering out from under his lashes. Candles made of the finest beeswax lit the room and gave off a clean scent reminiscent of meadow clover. The walls were whitewashed timber, and the windows diffused the afternoon sunlight. Ghost had never stood before the elders, and he suppressed a nervous giggle. The Eldest sat in the middle while the rest of the elders, usually eight in number, flanked him along one side of a long table built of deep-red Southron wood. One seat was empty.

"Speak," the Eldest commanded, his voice strong. He reminded Ghost of Merrah for an instant, the way his eyes seemed so much younger, despite the deep wrinkles of his weathered face.

"I am Ghost, witch and healer to the village, having been apprenticed to the Witch and found worthy by the witchsisters." Ghost spoke the formal words without stuttering, although his mouth was dry in the face of the influential elders. "I come before you to ask your help in a matter involving the entire village."

The man bowed his head to acknowledge Ghost's words and turned to Gerry. "Why are you here?"

Ghost knew the man was well aware of who Gerry was, but the words had to be said aloud so anyone there to witness events would hear as well. Today, with the epidemic raging, no one watched from the back of the room, but the formalities still needed to be observed.

"I am Gerry, an alpha of the village, so acknowledged by you, Eldest. Ghost is my sworn mate before the gods. I come to add my voice to his." Gerry's voice was strong and confident, and Ghost enjoyed a swell of pride in his mate.

The Eldest nodded. "Say what you have come to say, witch."

Ghost took a breath. "A malady is plaguing the village, the likes of which has not been recorded in the histories handed down to me by my predecessor. The illness spreads without regard to location or any other obvious means, and this malady afflicts both men and women, young and old. I believe we are facing an epidemic."

The elders shifted in their seats, uneasy. One man dropped his head in his hands, and the elder seated beside him leaned forward.

"One of the elders has fallen sick," the Eldest said in a grave voice. "I am told he has a fever and has been vomiting blood."

Ghost's mouth was dry as dust. "The oldest and the very young are most susceptible. I'll be very honest. I can treat the symptoms of the illness, but I can't cure the patient completely. Eleven people have died already." Ghost took another breath, his hands feeling damp. "I'm seeking a cure. But in the meantime, I think the wisest course of action is to create a central spot for treatment. I'm one witch, and I waste time going from street to street to treat patients and look for more afflicted. Give me an empty warehouse to use. I'll ask the alphas of the patients brought to the warehouse to bring bedding and contribute to feeding the sick."

"Who will help you, since you are just one witch?" The man next to the Eldest, on his right side, spoke.

"People who've been infected and have recovered seem to be immune. Two such women help me already, with the leave of their alpha. Merrah and her daughter, Mai." Ghost tried to remember to breathe as he waited for the Eldest to speak.

"You agree with the witch's request?" The Eldest shifted his attention to Gerry.

"I do. Ghost has been tireless in aiding the sick and seeking answers. He wears himself out trying to be in so many places at once. If I had the space in my own home, I'd offer him the use, Eldest. I agree with Ghost strongly." Gerry glanced over at Ghost in encouragement. "No witch could do more than he's done, and now the time has come for us to help him."

The Eldest nodded. "Give us a moment to confer." The rest of the elders concurred in murmurs, and the man who had hidden his face lifted his head, looking weary. The elders all looked tired, and Ghost realized the welfare of the village was as much their concern as his.

Gerry led him back out to the small antechamber, and Ghost took a deep breath.

"Father protect us, they're fucking scary," Ghost whispered.

Gerry clapped a hand over his own mouth to stifle a laugh. "They are," Gerry said, and Ghost relaxed as Gerry's hand cupped his cheek, a tender touch meant to reassure. "But you spoke well, and I think they'll agree. They still need to talk among themselves and settle matters in their own minds."

Ghost let Gerry pull him close, enjoying the feel of Gerry's arms around him. If the elders refused his request, he would need an alternative. He wondered if the godsman would consider letting him use the grounds of the gods' house. Tents were feeble protection as the weather grew colder, but they would be better than nothing. If the gods smiled on him, Ghost might find a solution long before the true cold set in.

"What are you thinking?" Gerry's breath was hot against his ear.

"I'm thinking we're going to make an awkward appearance before the elders when we go back in, if you keep holding me so close." Ghost regarded Gerry, pleased to see the answering glint of humor in his eyes. "And I'm thinking about other ways to house the sick if they say no."

"Use our house," Gerry said promptly. "At least for the worst cases. I can stay with Mother and Conn. I'll make sure you have plenty to feed them and lots of wood for the fires. I'll do what I can."

"I can't ask you to make such a sacrifice." Ghost felt a wave of love and gratitude. "I wouldn't even know how long I'd need to house them. I can't ask you to leave our house for an indefinite period of time."

"Don't forget an alpha provides what's needed. If using our house will keep you from running yourself ragged, then we'll use our house." Gerry brushed Ghost's white hair back off his shoulders.

"Thank you," Ghost whispered. "You take such good care of me, even when I don't think I need caring for, or when I'm too busy to think about what I need. I'm so lucky, love."

The creaking of the old door kept Gerry from responding. Ghost reached for his hand as they went back into the elders' chambers and took their places in front of the table.

"We have considered your request with great care. Will the warehouse be useful once you are finished using it as an infirmary? You see, we remember the old words too. Lore is not solely the province of the witchsisters." The Eldest watched Ghost with ageless eyes, the wrinkles in his face making his expression unreadable. "But even if the warehouse is no longer of use, is the loss a fair trade if lives can be spared? The epidemic is cruel, and none of us remember an illness taking such a form. So, the malady is a new thing, at least for us, and we would not have it said we did not care for our people."

Ghost tightened his grip on Gerry's hand. The Eldest was asking valid questions, and Ghost could not promise the warehouse would not retain whatever was causing the illness. He would not offer a lie solely to get the warehouse. He took a quick breath, prepared to answer. The Eldest spoke again before Ghost could respond.

"The red-doored warehouse on the edge of the market has been vacant since the goods left on the last caravans to the South. If the warehouse can never be used to store goods again, the loss is acceptable. The building is also suited to your needs, since the warehouse has a small well. The structure was distant enough from the public wells to require a private supply." The Eldest looked at Ghost, and his wrinkled face folded into a smile, or at least Ghost thought he smiled.

"We have a stock of blankets and cots used for the visiting caravan trade. You may have use of those for your infirmary, young witch. You will also be allowed as much in the way of healing herbs and spices as you require." The Eldest glanced at Gerry. "You are a good hunter. A runner or two will feed many, and I am sure others will offer what they can to help. May the Father protect you both, and the Seeker provide you with answers."

"Thank you, Eldest, and all of you elders." Ghost bowed his head, giddy with relief, but before he could turn to leave, the man seated at the right hand of the Eldest spoke.

"Had we not agreed, what would you have done, young witch?" The elder watched him with an expression Ghost could only call predatory.

"My alpha offered our house for the most afflicted. They'd have been given some dignity before their passing." Gerry's hand tightened around Ghost's.

The man turned to the Eldest. "You were right."

"I usually am," the Eldest replied and waved an age-spotted hand at Ghost and Gerry. "Go see to your infirmary. You will want to get the building ready, I am sure. We will have the cots and blankets brought there at once."

Ghost hesitated. "Eldest, can I ask? What were you right about?"

The wrinkled face folded again, creases collapsing into creases. "My young friend here did not think you had the mettle of your mentor. I told him if pressed, you would be just as quick to chastise us as she was. You did not disappoint, Ghost. I am quite pleased. It bodes well for our village to have such a determined witch."

Ghost could almost feel Gerry's amusement behind him. His cheeks grew warm as he turned and tugged Gerry with him as he hurried out.

Chapter Eight

GERRY AND GHOST left the chamber of the elders and strode across the market to the warehouse. Men arrived with the promised cots and blankets. Ghost designated a room for the infants and their dams, and a somewhat more spacious room for the elderly. He suspected the older patients would be the larger group. Ghost chose a workroom with a hearth for himself so he could keep heated water ready for both infusions and washing. A worktable suitable for preparing herbs stood against one wall, and chests for linens and other necessities flanked it.

Ghost asked for a single cot and a brazier to be placed in the small room tucked away in the back. Gerry gave Ghost a quizzical glance, but Ghost didn't offer an explanation. Instead, he added a stool and a little table before closing the door.

It was too late to move any of the afflicted, and Ghost still needed to contact Zereda to see if she knew anything more. He also wanted to tell her what he had learned from the Witch, brief though the contact had been. He even dared hope the Witch would reach out through the scrying mirror to him again, and he could find out what she had been about to say.

"Gerry?" Ghost waited until his mate turned around. "I'd like to go home. I can finish the rest tomorrow."

Gerry looked as though he was about to say something. He stopped, clearing his throat instead. "This plague will work out, Ghost. Isolating the sick will help, and you've reached out for solutions. Have you thought about asking if another witch might be able to come and help? Do you even do anything similar?"

"You mean asking for a witch to come here? To work with me?" Ghost looked at Gerry, wondering why he had not thought of the idea himself. Gerry had helped other alphas with building additions to a house, or repairing a fence when the work was too much for one family. Why should a witch not help another witch in the same manner?

"If witches will even work together," Gerry replied. "Another healer would ease the workload on you, and you could agree to return the favor if she ever needed it."

Gerry had proposed a sensible solution, and a weight lifted from Ghost's shoulders. "There's a witchsister here in the Heartlands, not too far from here. I don't really know her all that well, but I can ask her if she can help. She's been friendly whenever we've had contact." He twined his fingers around Gerry's and groaned. "I'll reach out to her after we eat something. I have to think about food for the infirmary too. For the patients."

"We'll take a look in the meat house to start. I can replace what you take easily enough. The runners are still fat from the harvest leavings and fallen nuts." Gerry led Ghost to the door of the warehouse. "After we eat, I want to ask Mother and Conn to help tomorrow with moving the patients. Maybe we can get Moran, and Torrance, and Perth from the mead house. Strong backs will move your patients quicker."

Ghost nodded, still thinking about what he had at home in terms of foodstuffs. "I have flour I can spare, some salt, and I can take a little of my yeast for bread. I want soft foods for the sick."

"We'll ask around and see what people will offer, too." Gerry sounded confident, and Ghost looked over at him. "The alphas will bring food for their own people. I'll ask Conn if he can spare some eggs."

"I'd appreciate it, love," Ghost said. "Conn and I get along well enough, but I still sort of freeze when I have to ask him for anything. I'll get past being nervous soon, I hope. I'm not nearly as tongue-tied and stupid with Mother, for some reason. I know Conn was afraid I was taking you away, and he was jealous. When Bernd had me, Conn tried to save me, and neither one of us is holding a grudge. At least I think we're not. I'm not."

"Mother's an alpha. You've no problem telling alphas what to do. You only get shy around dependents. Or hadn't you noticed? The way you stood up to Moran? Many words describe you, Ghost, but 'tongue-tied' and 'stupid' don't come close at all. Try 'fierce' and 'brave.'" Gerry's voice was warm with pride.

Ghost's cheeks heated. "I'm not, really. Fierce. I'm just not good at letting people behave like Moran did. And you noticed how he turned around when he found out Sari had a boy. I know his partner gave him daughters, but I don't see why a son was such a big deal."

"He's got one daughter who's as good with wood as he is." Gerry steered Ghost toward the street leading home. "A few alphas would like to court her."

"Did you ever?" Ghost asked. "Court any daughters?"

Gerry's eyes widened. "What brought this on?" He shook his head. "No, I've never had an interest in women. Some, like Mother, don't mind either way. Not me. The only company I've ever wanted is another man. You, my precious Ghost."

"So you'll never sire a child, then." Ghost did not quite understand the odd feeling in his stomach.

"Thinking about the babes?" Gerry stopped and turned Ghost around to face him, cupping Ghost's face in his hands. "The Witch herself would tell you, you can't save them all. I know you hurt when you see them losing the struggle and hear their dams crying. I don't know if I could bear having to watch. But at least you and I won't know such pain. Not the pain of losing a child of our bodies."

Ghost shrugged, uncomfortable with his own confusion. "I was remembering what I *saw*. But you know, the visions are all muddled up, and what I *see* isn't always what I imagine it is." He patted Gerry's chest and turned away, reaching for his hand. "Do you think we might take in a dependent or two? Sometime down the road?"

"Ghost," Gerry said, a world of concern in his voice.

Ghost stepped back and turned away, urging Gerry to walk. "At some point, I'll want to find an apprentice, you know. I'll want to pass on what I've learned. Someone needs to know all the lore I've accumulated, and how I've expanded on what I was shown. I want to hand down our traditions the way the Witch did with me. Even with as little as we do know, we witches can still make a difference." Ghost took a moment to swallow the lump in his throat before continuing. "I want to leave something behind. Maybe I won't leave a child sired and raised by us. But I want something to mark I was here and did my best to help."

"You're the first male witch in generations. You count for something. Your presence will be recorded by the witchsisters. Even though some of them hate you and would love to feed you to a lair full of hungry sind." Gerry's eyes held humor. "There are far more who'll make sure everyone remembers how the Witch taught Ghost, a witch and a seer, and a man of honor. I hope they mention your beautiful spiral. Those stones that glow when you're working your magic, but never shine brighter than your eyes."

Ghost coughed to hide the startled sob that almost escaped him. "Listen to you. You're all full of words, like the stories I used to read in the ruins. Compliments are very confusing, you know. I'm not used to thinking of myself as anyone special. The Witch used to tell me I'm not completely housebroken. I'm only me. I still make mistakes, and people make me nervous."

"Who's the alpha here?" Gerry said as Ghost chanced a sidelong glance at him. "You were special enough for me to fall in love with you the day I met you."

"You can blame that on the hemp. Good for pain, but gives you the oddest notions." Ghost could feel the smile starting on his lips. "Like thinking you're falling in love."

"And then I was so sure I'd scared you off when I asked you to stay with me in the bed. But waking up with you next to me felt so right." Gerry smiled at him. "You're all I want, beloved, more than enough for me. Even if we never have another dependent, it doesn't matter. I don't need anything more than you in my life. It's why I was so angry with the godsman's delay. I knew you were the one I was waiting for."

"But if we had a dependent? Would it ruin things?" Ghost's stomach twisted with tension. The vision had been muddled. He had seen a child, but the image had shifted so quickly. The child could have been anyone, or meant anything. The possibilities were endless, the reason unknown. Perhaps the vision was merely an arbitrary child or a symbol of something he did not yet understand. But part of Ghost wished the child was meant for him, even if just as an apprentice.

"Don't be silly. Having a dependent wouldn't ruin anything. I wouldn't be surprised if we did eventually take one in. Sort of like the Witch's friend winding up with an abandoned sind whelp. There are enough children who lose their place and are orphaned. I'd be crazy to think we wouldn't be happy with one of them as ours." Gerry led Ghost into the yard of their house.

The frost along the edges of the paving stones sparkled in the light of the moon. The sky was perfectly clear, but Ghost shivered anyway, feeling a chill creep up his spine.

Gerry tightened his hold on Ghost's hand. "You're freezing. Let's get inside, and we can have some of the good stew you made this morning. A bowl of something hot and you'll feel better."

Ghost let Gerry guide him through the door. "I think I'm just tired. I still want to try to reach a few of the sisterhood who were looking for answers. Maybe the Witch will contact me again. You never know. But I don't want to stay up too late. I'll be busy tomorrow, and I can take the mirror with me so I won't miss anything. And my notes. I'll need my notes and my formulary. And one jar I'll keep tucked away. The Seeker's rest." He glanced at Gerry, seeing puzzlement in his mate's gaze. "If I can't help them, and they ask me, I can ease the way. The tincture's not perfect, but I can offer a gentler death."

Gerry's expression made Ghost's heart sink a little. Fear, disappointment, and disapproval, all rolled into one.

"I've never made a secret of the fact some of the knowledge I have can be harmful. I have to learn what herbs can help, but I also need to know which ones can cause harm, or even kill. Like the rhymes they teach children about the fungi growing around the trees. Some are delicious and others can kill if you eat enough." Ghost splashed some water from the pump over his hands. "We take an oath to use what we know to help. Do you trust me to keep my oath?"

Gerry moved the stew closer to the hearth and added a few chunks of wood to the fire. "You have dangerous knowledge. What if they ask and change their mind? You can't undo the effects, can you?" He looked at Ghost, and Ghost wanted to run from the questions in Gerry's eyes.

"You don't give them the tincture the first time they ask. You talk to them, and you listen to what they're really saying. I'm not always good with people, but I understand this part, when they're facing death. Most of the time what they need is simply to have someone listen and hold their hand so they're not alone. Or they want you to ask the Seeker to turn her mate away, even though we both know it won't happen." Ghost poured out some cool water into cups. "And sometimes, they really can't bear the pain any longer. They're too close, and they see his dread face, and they *know*. They ask you to help, and you have to decide if they really mean what they're asking."

Ghost's hands trembled as he put the cups of water on the table. "You said you hoped you'd never have to kill anyone again. You said you wondered why everyone simply accepted what you did, why no one said anything. Did you stop to think I might have to wonder about the same thing? I gave two elderly people the Seeker's rest today. I watched as they held hands while the tincture worked. I watched them die. So how am I supposed to feel? Did I do what my oath promised, or am I no more than a killer?"

Gerry reached out and pulled Ghost close to him, wrapping his arms around his mate. "I didn't mean to imply anything. I didn't mean you're a killer. I just...well, how do you decide?"

Ghost buried his face in Gerry's shoulder, breathing in the scent of Gerry's leather tunic. He needed a moment to find his voice. "I don't decide. They do. I have to make sure they know what they're asking me for. And after they decide, I'm the one watching. I'm going to watch them die either way. The choice is how. It should be their choice, not mine. I shouldn't force them to die slowly, in pain, scared of what's happening, because I'm afraid to offer them a way out. I don't expect you to understand because I didn't really know either, until the first time I offered that choice. Today, as a matter of fact. So, I'm still working through how it feels myself."

"I'm sorry. I didn't think," Gerry murmured, but he sounded unconvinced.

Ghost slipped out of his arms. "Why don't you get the bowls down and dish out the stew?" Ghost said. His chest hurt so much he could barely breathe, and his lips felt numb as he formed the words. Gerry had said what Ghost did as a witch was his decision, but now Gerry thought he had made the wrong choice. Gerry thought he was a killer. "We'll eat, and I'll see who I can reach tonight. Afterward, I think I need to sleep. I have a lot to do tomorrow if I'm going to make this work. Are you still going to talk to Mother and Conn tonight?"

"I think I will, yes," Gerry replied, and the careful distance in his voice was vast enough to make Ghost's heart sink even more. "Ghost, don't think I don't trust you. But bringing about a death shouldn't be easy. I can't help but wonder if maybe the Witch made some of what you can do seem too easy, or if being raised apart the way you were had something to do with it. But I think you follow your oath the best you know how."

"Thank you. I think," Ghost said. He felt icy-cold inside, but his cheeks were on fire. "I suppose I'm on my own with this anyway. I'm the one who gets to listen and make the choice to offer to kill them before the illness does. Witch's business, right? No one will point a finger at you as long as you can pass off the blame. You can just say I did what I had to do."

"I said I'd trust you when it came to witch's business, didn't I? I suppose I have to make good on my word." Gerry sounded as bleak as Ghost felt, and for a moment, Ghost wanted to apologize. He yearned to tell Gerry everything was all right, and Gerry did not have to understand.

Instead, Ghost watched in silence as Gerry put the bowls of stew on the table. He realized in a hot rush he was angry at the condescension in Gerry's words, at how easily Gerry implied he had no empathy for people, no real understanding of what the healer's oath he had sworn meant. What other oaths did Gerry think Ghost had misunderstood? Their mating vow, maybe? Ghost remembered Gerry asking for his promise at the Witch's house that first day, and how Gerry had made Ghost feel like a person. Now Gerry had taken his confidence away with a few cruel words.

Ghost had needed all his courage to sit next to the two people who had asked for his tincture. He had given them the drops and watched as their breathing slowed. He had not moved, not until they were still. He had no doubt the Seeker's rest would be needed again, and no words to explain to Gerry why death could be a part of healing.

They ate in near silence, Gerry's fingers drumming on the tabletop. Ghost's appetite was nonexistent as he pushed the stew around in his bowl while he watched from under his lashes as Gerry ate. Ghost missed the ability to hide behind his long hair, worn bound back now to show his witchmark. Gerry did not glance up until the bowl was empty, but Ghost could not meet his eyes.

Gerry stood, placed his bowl in the stone tub, and left without a word. Only then did Ghost look up from his bowl of stew. He scraped the uneaten food into the slops bucket. He washed and dried the bowls and cups before putting them on the shelf.

Having stalled all he could, Ghost opened the drawer of his formulary cabinet and unwrapped his mirror with less than steady hands. Reaching the proper state of mind to send out his call took longer than usual, and even then, the pressure behind his spiral was sharper and angrier than normal. The night was quiet, far quieter than Ghost would have liked. He would have welcomed even Sri and her bitter mental sneer rather than this painful silence in his home and in his heart.

Ghost was close to admitting defeat when he felt the tug of contact and saw the blue crescent signaling Zereda's presence. More than mere relief coursed through him. The soft slur of her mental voice was the closest thing to comfort he could hope for this night.

"Little brother," Zereda began. "Did you find her?"

"She found me, actually, sister." Ghost sighed. "She asked me if it had started. The epidemic. As if she'd been expecting it."

"Odd, little brother. She is not a seer as we are. Could you tell where she was?" Zereda's mental voice was strained.

"She's in the Northlands. She said the problem started in the South, but the answer was there. She said something about having an answer, but the trick was going to be getting out. And she ended the contact without any warning. Fast enough to hurt when she broke our link."

The strain in Zereda's voice was stronger. "There is no choice, little brother. This was earlier this morning, yes?"

"Yes. I'd been in the village, doing what I could. I came home to wash before speaking to the elders. They've given me a warehouse to use for the sick."

Ghost's anxiety rose as he listened to Zereda. "She tried to reach me, not long ago. But before she spoke to you, I believe. She was looking for you, little brother. I heard fear in her voice, but the Witch I know is rarely frightened." Zereda paused. "You need to find her."

"She's in the Northlands, and it's close to winter. Travel north is impossible now." Ghost watched the blue crescent in his mirror grow sharper. "The passes will be blocked by snow. No caravan will be traveling this way, either. The last ones left already."

"You will move faster without a caravan, and witches' ways remain open. Not every traveler goes over the mountains, little brother." Zereda's voice carried gentle humor. "The time has come to share one of the secrets of our sisterhood, since the Witch has not done so. Tunnels with metal carriages run under the mountains ringing the Heartlands. Is your formulary a copy of hers?"

Ghost's stomach clenched. "Yes. She prepared it herself."

"Then we are in luck. Look for an entry for *velox iter*, which will tell you where to find the carriageway. The station will have instructions on how to charge the carriage and make it travel. The journey to the Northlands should take less than a hand of days." Zereda's voice was confident.

"And what about the sick here? What about my oath? 'Above all else, and before the gods, I will do no harm.' I said the words, Zereda. I can't leave them with no one to look after them." Ghost felt the heat in his spiral heralding the Seeker, and the touch of Sight. He pushed it away as best he could.

"Natali will come tomorrow at first light. You will know her by the starburst on her brow, as purple as the sunset. She will stand in as the witch for your village. You, Ghost, are the only one who has a chance of finding the Witch and any solutions she holds." Zereda was implacable.

"The Northlands is vast. I don't have the first clue where to look." Ghost offered a token protest. He could not refuse to search for the Witch. She had searched for him not so long ago, she and Gerry, along with Mother and Conn. "And I don't know what to tell Gerry. I can't just vanish. He's more than my alpha. He's my mate."

The words fell like stones even as they left Ghost's lips. He was no longer certain Gerry would care if he vanished. Or perhaps Gerry would try to forbid Ghost from leaving. He was not sure if his duty to the Witch and the village outweighed his obligations to his mate. But the Witch held answers. Ghost might not have to offer his tincture to anyone else.

"The Seeker will guide you," Zereda replied.

Ghost's stomach roiled from nervousness. Something had triggered this epidemic, and while the Witch thought she had a solution, Ghost could still seek the catalyst. He had Tal to contact. He would have time on the journey.

"One last thing, little brother. A guess, and no more. We have an insect here, a small annoyance, buzzing about and nipping at the flesh it can find. Sometimes, in the wake of its bite, there is a fever, followed by hemorrhaging from the mouth and nose. If a stomach flux were somehow added, well. The resulting malady sounds far too much like what you are seeing in the sick." Zereda hesitated. "I have heard rumors of relics in the West Reaches. Centrifuges can spin and combine the smallest of particles, such as phages or viruses, and place them in bacteria. You may find such rumors worth considering."

"Thank you, sister. I'll consider the rumors with care," Ghost replied. "But now, I need to go. I need to prepare if I'm going to leave tomorrow after Natali comes. This has to succeed, Zereda. If I don't find the Witch, I won't be able to come back, if I even survive the trip. I'm leaving my village in a crisis and walking out on my alpha and mate. I won't be forgiven."

"I know, little brother, but you are the only one who stands a chance of finding the Witch. Use the bond between you." Zereda's crescent faded away, and Ghost looked at the mirror, seeing the reflection of his spiral, angry and bright.

With a sigh, Ghost wrapped the mirror up to be packed. The gods' light and Seeker's kiss were both fed. Those he would take, as well, along with his formulary. His head ached, and Ghost reached for the hemp, wanting the deeper sleep the herb could provide. He would not have a chance to make things right with Gerry before he left, and his departure would probably make matters worse. He would look as though he was running from something too large to handle, a public admission he was not a proper witch. He did not bother to add honey to the infusion after he brewed it, barely registering the bitter taste as he contemplated the ruin he had made of his life.

Chapter Nine

GERRY WALKED UP the familiar path to the blue door of Mother's house. The door was partially open, as it usually was, so Gerry walked into the kitchen. He noted the tidy state of the place. Mother looked up from the chair by the fire with a quizzical expression.

"Lady smile on you," Gerry said as Mother rose.

"Conn, come and see Gerry," Mother called. He waved Gerry to sit at the table. "I'll pour us some mead."

Conn came out of the bedroom, dressed in loose linen pants and a light tunic, looking around as he spoke. "Hello, Gerry. Where's Ghost? He still in the village?"

Gerry's throat tightened. The last thing he wanted to do was to tell Mother how he had left things with Ghost. "He's home. He wanted to check some things. He asked the elders today for a place to use as an infirmary, and they gave him the old warehouse at the edge of the market."

"The one with the red doors?" Mother poured mead into three cups. "The building is hardly used these days anyway."

"Exactly. It'll be easier for Ghost to have all the worst cases in one place, and he thinks isolating the sick may slow the spread of the disease. But I came to ask if you'd have time tomorrow to help us shift the sickest patients to the warehouse." Gerry accepted the cup, watching Conn get some plump dates for them to enjoy. "I understand if you don't want to chance being around the plague."

"I had the sickness." Conn shrugged. "I was in the market trading eggs for some of the Southron goods, like these dates. Last Seaday, wasn't it?" He looked over at Mother and then back at Gerry. "The market was unusually crowded because the weather was so good. I felt like shit come nightfall, vomited a few times, and Mother said I was warm."

"You were as hot as a stone in the sun," Mother said. "But your teeth were chattering as though you were freezing."

Conn sat and sipped his cup of mead. "Anyway, I was fine by the next night. I think Fatherday was when you came down with it as well?"

Mother nodded. "The disease was much the same for me. A headache, vomiting for a full day, and a fever. I rested, and I was well again the next day."

"You rested because I all but tied you to the fucking bed," Conn said. Gerry heard the easy affection in his voice. "But anyway, I think we've already had whatever this plague is running through the village, although neither of us had any bleeding. Does Ghost know what's causing this disease?"

"Not yet." Gerry nibbled a date and was startled by the sweetness. He had forgotten the taste of the Southron fruit, and his first thought was how Ghost might like these. Then he remembered the look on Ghost's face, and his heart sank. "He's trying to figure the damned malady out, but it's been tricky. He's lost a couple hands of patients already, and he took it hard."

Mother must have picked up on something in Gerry's voice because he looked at him with a sharp expression Gerry knew all too well.

"If he took those losses hard, I'd think you'd not want to leave him. There's enough pressure on him because he's male and a witch." Mother's voice was soft, but Gerry heard the reprimand. "You're his alpha, Gerry. You can't walk away when the relationship gets uncomfortable."

"We had a stupid disagreement." Gerry forced himself to meet Mother's eyes as he made the admission. "Two of the villagers he found were old and hurting. They knew they weren't going to survive. Ghost knew they'd die too. He gave them a tincture he called the Seeker's rest that helped them to die peacefully. I wasn't sure how to deal with what he did. He killed them, strictly speaking."

Conn made a small sound and wrapped his hands around his cup. He looked as though he wanted to speak, but his dark-blue eyes were on Mother as he waited for his alpha, to Gerry's surprise. Conn of old would not have been so circumspect.

"Do you think those two people would have been better off dying while vomiting up nothing but blood?" Mother looked at Gerry and sighed. "I watched my dam make the same offer to those she couldn't help. I watched her sit with them, and hold their hands, and speak to them until they fell asleep. Sometimes it was the first time in days they looked peaceful, without pain. They could meet death on their terms. Some refused the Seeker's rest, of course, and my dam cared for them with the same tenderness until they died. After a while, you stop hearing the moans."

Gerry felt the tightness in his throat again. "I know the guilt a man has to carry when he's taken a life. I wanted to keep Ghost from having to endure what I do."

"Did you tell him, or even listen to him?" Mother asked. "Ghost did nothing any witch would find objectionable. They deal in death daily. They're not as afraid of dying as we are."

Gerry looked into his mead for a moment. "I told him it was witch's business. I dismissed his feelings and left him sitting there."

"It's ironic how we can get it so spectacularly wrong at times with the one we love the most. Of course, some of us take a few tries to figure this out." Mother looked over at Conn, and the younger man ducked his head. "Eventually, we do figure things out, Gerry. You can mend this with your Ghost."

Conn cleared his throat. "And to get back to why you came, I can bring some eggs tomorrow to the warehouse if you can use them. As a matter of fact, I have a pair of productive hens I can spare if you and Ghost want more eggs yourselves."

"I'll say yes to both, although Ghost will probably send over some liver loaf or a batch of scones as a thank you." Gerry held up his hand to still any protests. "I'm pretty sure Ghost understands gifts, but he feels like he should give something as well. Honestly, sometimes I think he really is an alpha. He's as stubborn as one, anyway."

Gerry finished his mead and declined any more with a small wave when Conn offered the bottle. "I should get back home and see about mending things with Ghost." He stood, reaching out to clasp Mother's hand in gratitude. He hugged Conn, Conn returning the embrace. "Take care of him," Gerry said quietly, meaning Mother, and Conn murmured acquiescence.

Gerry did not rush back to his house, though, despite what he had said to Mother and Conn. He needed a walk and time to clear his head. Ghost took matters to heart more than Gerry, and Ghost would likely have seen this as a lack of trust on Gerry's part. Add in Ghost's anxiety about failing in the face of this epidemic, and Gerry had a recipe for disaster.

The door to the house was closed when Gerry got home, although he could see a thin wisp of smoke from the hearth fire's chimney. The kitchen was dark, the lamps extinguished, but the glow of the hearth was enough to see by. Gerry took his boots off and left them by the door, padding over the wooden floor in silence.

The bedroom door was open, and Gerry could make out Ghost's body under the quilt. Ghost did not stir, which meant one of two things. Either he was upset and pretending to be asleep to avoid talking to Gerry, or he had made himself one of his infusions to help him sleep. In either case, he would not be talking to Gerry.

Gerry stripped and slid under the quilt before he grew chilled. He reached out and felt Ghost's knitted tunic. The linen breeches Ghost also wore formed a silent rebuke, and Gerry sighed. He had not been forgiven in his absence, and making amends would be even more of a challenge in the morning.

Nonetheless, Gerry wrapped his arms around Ghost. Ghost was so deep in sleep Gerry knew he had taken something. Probably the hemp he had used on Gerry to allow Gerry to sleep through the pain of a broken leg. Gerry's heart ached as he buried his face in the silken white hair and breathed in the scent of his Ghost as he watched the moon cross half the sky. Ghost never moved once in his embrace.

GERRY WOKE JUST past dawn. The bed was cold and empty. He sat up, scrubbing his fingers through his hair as he yawned and stretched. He tossed back the quilt and found his discarded breeches, not bothering to lace them all the way as he left the bedroom.

Ghost was in the main room, speaking to a woman, a starburst in rich purple marking her forehead and identifying her as a witch. He looked up as Gerry emerged, his face impassive. "You're awake," he said.

Gerry blinked a little. "I'm sorry," he said. "I didn't realize anyone would be here. My apologies, good witch." He reached for his laces in haste.

"This is Natali," Ghost said. "She'll be dealing with the patients in the infirmary. My sister, this is Gerry, my alpha."

Natali smiled at Gerry. "Lady smile on you, good alpha. I won't trouble you long. Ghost is giving me certain instructions, and I'll be on my way to the village."

"Mother and Conn will be by to lend a hand in moving the patients you want sent to the warehouse," Gerry said, addressing Ghost. He offered a quick and fervent prayer to the Moon, wanting Ghost to look back with more than the careful, neutral expression he reserved for strangers. "Conn's going to bring another pair of chickens for the coop, as well as extra eggs for the infirmary. I thought I'd wash up and see if I can get Moran and Torrance, and maybe a few others to help too."

"Thank you," Ghost replied, but his expression didn't warm. "Natali will be at the warehouse, waiting." He paused, and Gerry wished they were alone so he could plead his case with Ghost.

Ghost, however, did not seem as eager to talk.

"I'll go wash, then." Gerry returned to the bedroom to gather clean clothing and a towel. When he came back out, Ghost was gone.

Washing did not take Gerry long, and he stopped only for a quick drink of water before he went to find some strong backs to help move the sick. Moran's house was his first stop. As he walked through the village, he noticed chalk marks on some of the doors, although Moran's door was unmarked. Moran was quick to agree to help and was able to offer an explanation of the chalk marks. Ghost had been along already this morning, at dawn, marking the doors of the sick needing to be moved to the infirmary.

All through the village, people were aware of the new infirmary, and the unfamiliar word was on everyone's lips. Plenty of volunteers arrived from among the healthy villagers. Gerry was surprised how many of them told the same tale as Mother and Conn, a brief brush with the illness and back to solid health. They had no fear of dealing with the sick people.

As they moved people, Gerry wondered where Ghost had gone, but there was no time to look. Conn had found a young and very pregnant woman in the last throes of the plague, blood dripping from her nose and mouth.

When they delivered her to the infirmary, Natali directed Mother and Conn to take the woman to the room with the infants. Gerry looked at her in confusion, and Natali sighed. "She might give birth, and it's better for her to be with other women who'd recognize the early signs of labor far faster than a room full of old men."

Gerry saw the sense in Natali's decision. A chance existed, slim but still a chance, the babe would be strong enough to survive. Plenty of dams who had lost babes would be happy to nurse an infant and maybe offer the child a home.

High sun came and went before Gerry had an opportunity to take a break. Conn had brought a large pot of soup as well as the promised eggs. Mai and Merrah helped to feed the sick, both of them gentle and kind as they made sure everyone had at least something warm. Natali prepared the infusion Ghost had given her according to his instructions and made her rounds of her patients.

Gerry accepted a bowl of soup from Mai. "Have you seen Ghost anywhere?" he asked.

"I haven't, actually. He was here earlier. I'd swear by the Lady he was." Mai frowned. "I saw him marking doors very early, and he asked if I could help. Have I seen him since then?" Her frown deepened as she thought back.

"No matter. I'll find him." Gerry smiled to set Mai at ease. After a quick word to Natali, he left the warehouse to look for Ghost.

Gerry cut through the market, the streets far too quiet, with far too many of the traders missing. He wondered how many were ill and how many were merely afraid. He wandered through the surrounding streets, seeing a great many smudged chalk marks but no Ghost. The volunteers had taken to smearing the chalk on houses they had visited, and only a few untouched marks remained. Gerry decided to head back home, hoping Ghost had perhaps returned there.

Ghost was leaving the house as Gerry entered the yard. He was wearing a heavy leather tunic and breeches with tall boots. A leather pouch was slung over Ghost's right shoulder and a water skin over the left. Ghost held the fur cloak Gerry had made, his pale face expressionless.

"Ghost?" Gerry said, and he could hear the uncertainty in his own voice. "I was hoping we could talk."

Ghost shook his head, and he took a deep breath before he met Gerry's eyes. "I have to go."

"Where?" Gerry asked. "When were you going to tell me?" He took a few steps forward, closer to Ghost. "Can't we talk before you run away?"

"I'm not running away." Ghost's voice was sharp. "Seeker guide me, you're making this harder. I need to find the Witch. I need the answers she has."

"You said yourself she's in the Northlands," Gerry protested. "The passes are all snowed in by now. There's no way you can get through on your own." Gerry held up his hand as Ghost opened his mouth. "I'm not saying this because I think you're helpless or weak. A caravan is lucky to come out of those passes with anyone still alive once the snows have started. You won't even have the protection of wagons and tents and other warm bodies."

"I'm a witch, Gerry. We have our own ways of doing things. I can get to the Northlands well enough." Ghost's voice was flat. "Did you see the pregnant woman? She's reached the point where I'm pretty sure I can't save her. *Them.* We're going to lose her and her unborn babe. Who'll be next? Women who've just given birth and who've seen their babes die? Will they succumb next? I have to do this. I know no one will understand, not even you, but I have to do this."

"How are you going to find one woman in the Northlands? It's vast, Ghost. You could wander for years and not find her." Gerry dared to reach out, but his fingers barely brushed Ghost's cheek before Ghost flinched away. "Ghost."

"You questioned me for trying to ease death for some of the dying. Look at it this way. I won't be killing anyone while I'm gone." Ghost's voice held enough bitterness to make Gerry's stomach tighten. "Maybe by the time I come back, you'll have found it in your heart to forgive me, or to at least understand why I did what I did. In the meantime, you'll have Natali to care for the sick. She might use the Seeker's rest too, but you won't hold those deaths against her like you do me. It won't bother you so much if it's not your dependent doing the killing."

"Ghost, I don't think you're a killer. I was wrong," Gerry said. His heart ached. Ghost had said *dependent*. Did he believe Gerry no longer saw him as his mate? Gerry had no way to know, and the pain hit him like a blow. "I was a fucking blind idiot. I wish I could unsay the words, but I can't. I'm sorry, Ghost. I'm so fucking sorry. Please don't go."

"I'm not leaving because you don't trust me or because we've argued. I have to go because no one else can find the Witch but me. I don't have a choice." Ghost's pale-blue eyes searched Gerry's face. "I can *see* her when no one else can. She put this witchmark on me, stone by stone. We're linked in a way no one else can match."

"Then let me go with you," Gerry said. He reached for Ghost again, and this time Ghost did not pull away. Gerry held him close, letting out a shaky breath as he buried his face in Ghost's hair. "We'll find her together."

"If you leave with me, they'll say we both ran away," Ghost said, his voice muffled in Gerry's cloak. "If you're here, they might believe I'll come back. Please, Gerry. I need to go alone. We talked about this. You said you would let me go if I needed to. I need you to be strong enough to let me leave."

"Can you promise me you'll come back?" Gerry lifted Ghost's chin and searched his eyes with desperate urgency. "Did you *see* yourself back home with me?"

"*Seeing* doesn't work that way. I *see* what the Seeker shows me. Most of the time, the vision barely makes sense. I'd have given anything to *see* me coming home to you, but I'd be lying if I said I did." Ghost did not look away from him.

Because he could think of nothing better to do, Gerry kissed Ghost. The kiss was tender and full of the grief Gerry could not find words to describe, and his throat ached with the effort of holding back another flurry of pleading.

Ghost returned the kiss, fingers sliding into Gerry's hair.

"Come back," Gerry said when they finally broke apart. "Don't promise, because I know you can't. Tell me you want to come back to me."

"More than anything," Ghost whispered, and Gerry could hear sorrow in his voice. "I love you. I'm sorry I can't be perfect. But I do love you. Now…"

"I don't need you to be perfect, beloved." Gerry's voice broke. "I need you to be my Ghost."

Ghost moaned, raw and full of pain. He shook his head, one hand splayed against Gerry's chest. "Please, Gerry. Let me go before I forget how to be strong enough to do this."

Watching Ghost walk away was harder than Gerry thought possible. When he did not look back, Gerry had to force himself to stand still. He watched until Ghost disappeared from sight. Gerry sighed and turned back toward the house with a hollow ache in his heart.

Chapter Ten

GHOST COULD FEEL Gerry's stare at his back, but he could not turn around. He would drop his pouch and water skin and run to the safety of Gerry's strong arms. He knew he would. Ghost had forgiven Gerry with one look in those eyes he loved. For a moment, he contemplated abandoning this futile quest and remaining here, with Gerry, to deal with the epidemic as best he could on his own. But he steeled his will and offered a silent promise, or maybe it was a prayer. *The Witch holds the solution and my duty is to seek her out. To save lives. I will return to you, love. Hold me in your heart until you hold me in your arms again.*

Ghost shouldered his pouch and walked the path to the Witch's house. He had told Natali how to find the Witch's house so she would have a place to stay if she needed some respite from tending the sick of the village. It was a perfect place for a witch, after all, and she could use the witchglass there to feed her own gods' light. For himself, the path would take him along the edge of the ruined city where he had hidden when young and heartsore.

A peculiar sense of loss enveloped Ghost as he walked past the yard. He had spent most of his life in this small house with the Witch. She had been everything to him for so long. Perhaps she had not been the warmest of people, but she had made sure Ghost knew he had a home with her. When he had shown an interest in her lore, the Witch had taught him with unexpected patience. Her home had been a haven for a lonely boy filled with visions. Just for a moment, he let himself have the luxury of wanting to be the Witch's apprentice once more, free from the weight of the sick and the dying.

The formulary indicated the station was located outside the ruins, north and west of the former city. Ghost decided to take the trail that skirted the ruins. What was left of the city was unstable and often impassable due to collapsed buildings.

Prudence also dictated he avoid the ruins, although Ghost knew several paths through the city itself. As Gerry had pointed out, he was alone, and exiled rangers prowled the ruins. While they were generally more intent on scavenging what relics they could, he was not willing to take more risks than strictly necessary.

From this vantage on the outskirts, Ghost was reminded the city must have been breathtaking when it was still thriving and vital. The ravages of time and scavenging had left their mark, and many of the buildings had all but crumbled to the ground. Still, enough of the city remained to spark imagination. The Witch had shown Ghost a book once, with crystal-clear images of the cities, the tall buildings lit with glowing points of light like an array of stars.

But Ghost needed to get to the station, and he could not afford to waste time. The epidemic was not going to wait while he had foolish Sea dreams. The path was obscure by design, but the witchmarks were there if one knew how to read them. Ghost navigated his way through the undergrowth of the forested area, keeping the ruins to his right side.

The afternoon wore on as Ghost walked, and the shadows of the trees danced as the sun dropped closer to the horizon. Going by the witchmarks, he had a way to go yet, and night would fall before he arrived at the station. He did not like the idea of camping alone out in the open, so he decided to push onward. The moon was bright enough, and he would find his way.

Despite having a good idea of where he was going, Ghost came close to missing the station. The entrance was overgrown, and even autumn had not removed the thick layer of vines camouflaging the entryway. If a stray bit of moonlight had not glinted off the door at exactly the right angle, Ghost might have passed it by.

The formulary had provided a code to be input on the pad of buttons by the entry. The moment Ghost touched the pad, light flared, and he pulled his hand back in surprise. He huffed a small breath in relief when nothing else happened, and he pressed the buttons in the correct sequence. He took a step backward as the door slid open, disappearing into what looked like a solid rock wall.

"Seeker guide me," Ghost whispered. He stepped into the opening, flinching when a line of lights appeared along the bottom of the wall on either side, illuminating part of a flight of stairs leading down. Ghost took the first few steps with caution. As he descended, the lights in front of him extended farther ahead, while the lights behind him blinked out. The door slid closed, leaving Ghost to decide if he wanted to continue down or to try to open the door again.

No dust gathered on the stairs, and the air was fresh and cool, which did not make him feel any more secure. Someone kept the station in order, and he had no desire to meet them. Ghost mustered all his nerve to keep going forward. If he went back, he could not guarantee he would not flee back to the village.

The floor leveled out at last, the faint lights along the walls spreading outward to indicate a larger space than the stairs. Ghost took a deep breath and reached out a hand. The walls were cool, polished stone. The upper line of lights expanded at a rapid pace, and the increased illumination seemed almost too bright after the dim trip down the stairs.

"Hello?" Ghost's voice echoed off the smooth walls. "Lady smile on you, from a traveler."

Ghost waited in silence for a long moment. A soft chime followed by a female voice echoed through the room, the words unintelligible, repeated over and over at increasing speed.

"Hello?" Ghost tried again.

"Hello. Welcome to terminal station nineteen. Please proceed to the main terminal." The female voice was soft, the words cadenced in an unfamiliar way, but finally understandable.

What the words might mean was something else altogether. Ghost took out his formulary, hoping for a bit of guidance. The journal's entry offered only a partial explanation, directing him to a main room where he could find a map. He glanced up from his book and noticed lights in the floor itself were pulsing green, as if to guide him in a specific direction. Having no better notion, he followed the lights into a much larger room, the vaulted ceiling almost invisible in the gloom beyond the reach of the lights.

To Ghost's relief, a large map occupied most of one wall, and he walked over to examine the display. The map bore little resemblance to the Witch's drawings in the sandy soil when he was a boy, and he frowned as he peered at it. Several lines in bright colors traversed the map, with small points on the lines marked by tiny glass domes. One point was flashing, and he read the symbols with care. Terminal station nineteen. Ghost wondered if it was possible the flashing light signaled his present location. With the bit of information and his theory, he was able to make out what had to be the ring of mountains forming the boundary of the Heartlands. His finger followed the line upward, past the ring, and into a rising crest of mountains.

"The Northlands," Ghost whispered.

"Please repeat. Terminal station the Northlands not recognized." The female voice sounded closer, and Ghost stepped away from the map in haste, casting around like a runner scenting sind.

He was still alone in the large room, and he waited until his heart had settled down to a more normal rhythm before he stepped close to the map again. He examined the small domes punctuating the line leading north, each dot with its own bit of writing in the ancient symbols. He bit back a sigh of disappointment as he looked at them. The map was not going to have a legend saying "The Witch is here." His eye caught a subtle difference, and Ghost leaned closer.

One dome had a faint smudge on it, as if a finger had brushed over it. Ghost felt a charge of excitement. He read the words next to the smudged dome and nodded to himself.

Stepping back from the map, Ghost said, "Terminal station eight." He felt silly speaking to thin air, but apparently the station did not agree.

"Terminal station eight. Departure is imminent from substation three. Please proceed to the substation." The female voice was cool and unruffled, and Ghost fought the urge to look around again.

Instead, Ghost glanced at the lights in the floor. A flashing green line urged him to walk farther into the room. The hesitancy Ghost felt earlier was giving way to curiosity, and he followed the green line through an archway and down a corridor. Featureless black panels were set into the walls here. Ghost thought one or two might have flickered as he went past, but he did not linger to investigate.

The green lights stopped at a large symbol on the floor. Ghost recognized it as the ancient number mark for three. He noticed a channel with a luminescent edge, set in the floor. An inky-black tunnel loomed at the far end of the channel. He started to walk closer to the edge, seeing a faint glimmer in the depths of the tunnel, but he did not quite reach the mark. Instead, he froze as a silver barrel—a carriage, Zereda had said—flashed into sight and stopped along the edge of the floor with a gentle hiss.

The front end of the carriage was tapered, almost elegant, with a brilliant white light at the tip. A door in the side slid open, much as the door on the surface had opened, revealing the inside of the carriage. Ghost moved closer, cautious, peering inside at the comfortable-looking benches and the soft lighting.

"Please step into the car. Departure is imminent." The female voice startled Ghost, and he stepped into the carriage without thinking. The door slid closed, and Ghost found himself off balance as the voice continued. "Please be seated for departure."

Simple reflex made Ghost obey and sit, and the carriage began to move forward. The walls had a row of flat black panels, smaller versions of those on the walls of the station, but the panels were equally blank. The carriage hummed and picked up speed, and Ghost had to swallow hard several times while he tried to adjust to the sensation of moving while sitting still. Ghost shuddered as he took in the lack of windows, almost as unsettling as mysterious voices from nowhere in the station. He had no idea where he was, or if he was going to the right place. Even if he had windows, he would not have known any more, he told himself.

After a time, the carriage settled into a steady motion. Ghost took a deep breath and decided to explore. Getting the carriage to move had taken little beyond choosing where he wanted to go, but Zereda had mentioned feeding the carriage. He wondered if the process was similar to feeding his gods' light or Seeker's kiss. If so, he would need a source of energy like his witchglass. Perhaps the panels on the wall were such a source? Zereda was confident he would find out, and Ghost decided to trust her wisdom.

Ghost took off his warm cloak and left it on a bench, along with his water skin and leather pouch. He walked over to a desk against one wall, cautious at first. A pad occupied part of the desk. He touched the smooth surface, and the pad lit almost at once. Several words appeared. He had to puzzle them out, but he finally decided they were "Illumination," "Information," and a last thing called "Menu."

Taking a chance, Ghost poked Menu. So far, nothing had seemed too dangerous, and he was interested to see what would happen. Images of various foods or meals appeared. He tapped one at random and waited to see what occurred. The pad flashed, and Menu flickered and disappeared, leaving only the other two choices. Ghost did not find this much of a surprise, since food would hardly have survived all this time. He had provisions he had brought, and he could trade for more once he reached the Northlands.

Caught up in the spirit of exploration, Ghost tugged on the bench. It unfolded into a bed with a padded surface. He found pillows and blankets stored in a cabinet behind the bench. A door in the rear of the carriage led to a cramped washhouse. Ghost puzzled out the proper place to take a piss and went back out to take a few swallows from his water skin.

The long walk and the excitement of discovering the tunnel had taken a toll on Ghost, though, and exhaustion began to win over curiosity. He pulled off his boots and settled down, wishing Gerry was with him. Ghost was not at all sure this carriage would take him to the Northlands, and he still had no idea what he would find should he reach his destination. The Witch could be anywhere, and loneliness threatened to overwhelm Ghost as he closed his eyes and tried to sleep. The steady hum of the carriage served to remind Ghost of how much he missed Gerry, and he drifted into an uneasy slumber, his dreams a jumble of Gerry's face and endless snow.

Chapter Eleven

GERRY CLOSED THE door on the darkness of the night. The house was far too quiet without Ghost.

He had been busy all day and into the evening, but Gerry found time to dwell on how Ghost had left as he changed his shirt and scrubbed his hands before leaving the infirmary. They had not had a chance to really talk, and Gerry wished he could relive the previous night. He would have given almost anything to take back his harsh words. Recalling the hurt in Ghost's eyes was unbearable.

Natali had given the Seeker's rest to an elderly woman this afternoon. Gerry knew the woman by sight but not well enough to know her name. Her neighbors had brought the woman to the infirmary. The persistent hemorrhaging marking the later stages of the plague was clear evidence she was dying. By chance, Gerry was standing there when Natali offered the Seeker's rest. He saw the look of gratitude in the woman's eyes, and she drank the tincture with a tired smile. Natali sat at the side of the bed, holding the woman's hand and speaking to her in a quiet voice until the woman fell asleep. Gerry watched them both for a few moments before he realized the woman was no longer breathing. He remembered Ghost's words as he watched and was ashamed.

The woman's passing was a sharp contrast to Bran's death. Gerry knew him well. Bran worked with Perth at the mead house. Bran cried out in agony with even the smallest movement, and he hemorrhaged from the mouth and nose. Bran turned down the Seeker's rest three times. Natali stopped offering the tincture after the third time. Instead, she bathed Bran's forehead and did her best to comfort him as he weakened from blood loss. He died sobbing, his voice ragged. Gerry was ashamed of the relief the man's death brought.

The shame did not lessen when Natali brought Gerry a cup of hot broth and a piece of bread. She said nothing, but her quiet sympathy reminded Gerry of how he had slighted Ghost. Ghost had not deserved the lack of trust Gerry had shown, and Gerry had not shown the proper behavior of an alpha. He had broken his promises to Ghost. Now Ghost had gone to look for the Witch alone, on a fool's mission to the wild Northlands. Gerry could only wait and pray to the Father to protect Ghost.

Gerry sat at the scrubbed wooden table in the tidy kitchen, seeing Ghost everywhere he looked. Ghost had insisted the witches knew a way to reach the Northlands. Gerry did not doubt his witch, but he also did not know if Ghost would be in danger on the journey. He was no fool. Gerry knew witches used the relics of the ancients, and those devices were a large part of their so-called magic. But Gerry had seen Ghost after a vision, and he had seen Ghost's visions realized. The ability to *see* was not something picked up in a ruin. The Sight was true magic, and Ghost had that power. What if Ghost's magic attracted something darker? What if the Witch's message had been meant to lure Ghost into a trap?

Gerry wondered if he could ask Natali to reach Ghost through her mirror, the way Ghost had reached out to the witchsisters. Wherever Ghost was, if Gerry could just know Ghost was well and uninjured, he could rest easier. He could not hope to be forgiven so easily and he could not ask, not over a scrying mirror with someone else to say the words. The right words were so hard to find to begin with, and Gerry wondered why it was so difficult. He had had no trouble using words to hurt Ghost.

He stood, his heart heavy. Walking into their bedroom was an effort, the bed cold and too large without Ghost to help fill the space, but Gerry needed to sleep. The day had exhausted him more than hunting or working guard ever had. Gerry had also gained a new perspective. Ghost's strength might not have been visible to the casual observer, but Ghost had been tireless over the course of the illness. One day had worn Gerry out. Ghost had managed for nearly a half moon without complaint.

Gerry did not bother to undress all the way. He stayed awake long enough to remove his boots and peel off his tunic. He crawled under the quilt and reached for Ghost's pillow. He wished he held Ghost in his embrace instead as he fell into a troubled sleep, missing his precious Ghost.

A GROWING LIGHT woke Ghost, and he reached for Gerry, hoping to bury his face in Gerry's shoulder and steal a few more minutes of sleep. His hand encountered a cabinet door, and he remembered he was not home.

Ghost threw off the blanket and yawned as he sat up. The panels along the wall emitted the imitation of daylight that had woken him from a restless sleep, although he felt no more rested than when he had closed his eyes. Some dried fruit and water from his stores made for a scant breakfast.

Ghost found himself missing the sound of Gerry moving about and humming to himself. Since he had joined Gerry to create their family, Ghost had become accustomed to the sound of voices. He and the Witch had gone for days without speaking aloud, but Gerry liked to talk, and Ghost missed the comfort of his mate's chatter.

He wandered back over to the desk to examine the pad again. The three options from the night before were still there, along with a new one reading "Power." Ghost wondered if this was the way to recharge the carriage.

Ghost pressed the new symbol. A green bar pulsed on the wall panel above the desk. Ghost regarded the panel with satisfaction. If the carriage worked on the same principle as the relics, the conveyance was gathering power.

Menu reappeared, and Ghost touched an image, expecting nothing to happen. The pad hummed, and the desk's top slid away, allowing a platform to rise up. Ghost found himself looking at a cup of hot, brown liquid.

"Seeker guide me," Ghost muttered, taken aback. The cup was real, its contents hot, but Ghost had no inclination to taste the strange drink that smelled sharp, more bitter than an infusion of hemp.

Ghost tried Information and a flurry of symbols filled the pad. He frowned as he attempted to read the unfamiliar words, until he resorted to the trick the Witch had taught him. He picked apart each word, looking for smaller, more recognizable words. One word looked familiar enough, and Ghost touched the symbol alongside it. The panel above the desk flickered, and a map appeared. The station in the Northlands was glowing green, and his point of origin was yellow. A small red dot traveled along the line, and Ghost was almost certain he could see the speck of color moving.

Tapping the red dot got him a small line, which Ghost read aloud. "Speed approximately five hundred kilometers per hour." Ghost had no notion of what a kilometer was, but he knew the carriage was traveling at impossible speeds if he could see movement on the map. This time of year, with the passes already getting snow, the notion was both welcome and disturbing.

Ghost had not taken the time to look at the map in the station at length, but he had nothing better to do to pass the time here in the carriage. The circles marking stations were near to, or in, the ruined cities. Lines representing tunnels linked the stations. It was simple and straightforward, and useless to Ghost. The world had changed too much since it was drawn. He left the map visible, though. If all else failed, he could watch the red dot move.

Ghost was restless. He needed to move, but he was, for all intent and purpose, trapped on this carriage. He could do nothing but speculate and worry. To occupy himself, he looked around the carriage for anything that might be useful. A section in the front held a familiar mark. He dropped to his haunches, looking at the crimson lines, thick and vibrant against the white background, one bisecting the other in an ancient healers' mark.

Ghost tugged on a small ring folded flat against the wall. A container slid out. Ghost heard a click, and the lid of the container rose enough for him to slip his fingers beneath the edge, and lift the lid up the rest of the way.

"Moon shine on me," Ghost murmured. The container overflowed with healers' supplies. He spotted rolls of bandages, liquids, ointments, salves, and small cylinders for his Seeker's kiss. Best of all, a new and gleaming gods' light and several pristine Seeker's kisses rested in soft packing.

Ghost's hand was trembling as he picked up treasure after treasure, unable to believe this stroke of luck. He put all the supplies in a large pouch he found under the lid of the container. At the very least, he could give Natali a Seeker's kiss for her aid. If the gods smiled on him, Ghost could have found one of the fabled antibiotics or vaccines the ancients used. He could be holding the cure to save his patients. Of course, he would need to get back to his village to test the supposition, if there was even a village left.

For now, though, Ghost had little to do except rest or try to read through the contents of Information. He felt guilty to be relaxing like this when his village was in the throes of an epidemic. He wanted to be doing something more tangible. His eye settled on the gleam of a curved section of the carriage, and Ghost groaned as he thought of what he could be doing. The ability to scry was not hampered by location, and he could not imagine his speed would do much to hinder him, either. He could reach out to Tal and see what she could tell him.

Ghost pulled the scrying mirror out and settled on the bench. He focused on the flawless surface and cleared his mind of everything but the witchmark Tal bore, knotwork in red. He did not expect an immediate response, and he let himself drift in a meditative state of relaxation while he waited.

GERRY HURRIED TO the village as the sun rose over the horizon, the grass still wet with dew. The market was stirring to life, and everything seemed peaceful and as normal as could be expected in the middle of an epidemic as he headed for the infirmary.

Visions of Ghost alone in some forsaken snowy pass, trapped and unable to go forward or back, or suffering with a broken leg, had haunted Gerry's sleep all night. The predawn sky had been a welcome sight, and he jumped out of bed with a sense of relief. He decided he had to ask Natali's help in reaching Ghost. He could not bear spending any more time wondering if his beloved Ghost was safe.

"Gerry!" Conn called out, and Gerry stopped, waiting for him to catch up. "Are you heading to the infirmary? I'll walk with you. I'm going there myself."

Gerry assented. "I need to speak to Natali to see if she can reach Ghost for me."

"He's gone, then?" Conn gave Gerry a sympathetic glance. "Did you get a chance to talk before he left?"

"Not really." Gerry shrugged one shoulder.

"I can cover so Natali can help you." Conn reached past Gerry to open the red door. "I'll clean up and hold a hand or two. You talk to Ghost."

THE PRESSURE BEHIND Ghost's spiral signaled contact. The scrying mirror clouded and a witchmark formed. He did not expect Natali's mark, and anxiety flooded him.

"I'm glad I reached you, brother." Natali's mental voice was sweet. "How are you? No, I'm sorry, *where* are you? Your Gerry is here and fretful."

"I'm happy to hear from you, sister," Ghost replied, speaking aloud to break the silence. The sound of his own voice was startling in the otherwise quiet carriage. For a moment, he thought he heard an echo, which did not seem possible in the small space. "I'm well, honestly, and as to where? I found the station, but I can't pinpoint where I am."

Ghost could feel hesitation in Natali's response. "Ah, good. Then you're well. Gerry was worried. The Sea sent him some disturbing dreams last night. He saw you injured or dying in the snow."

"If you tell Gerry not to share the knowledge, you can tell him about how I'm traveling. He understands witch's business can't be talked about too much. Besides, I'm only going to tell him myself, so you might as well. It'll ease his mind." Ghost settled himself on the bed in a more comfortable spot. "How are the patients doing? Have many more been brought in?"

Natali's voice took a moment to come back to Ghost. "I explained to Gerry about the carriages. He was a bit put out you didn't tell him before you left."

"I'd never been on one." Ghost was indignant, and he knew his reaction was clear to Natali. "I didn't even know if the thing was still working, much less what to expect. I can't tell him if I don't know. Can I?"

After the requisite pause, Natali replied, sounding amused. "He says he's sorry. And to bear with him because he's a simple hunter and not a brilliant witch like his mate." Her voice grew more somber. "We lost two yesterday, and the babe you were fretting over worsened overnight. I'm not holding out hopes for him. An older man came in, right at the beginning stages. He's responding as well as I'm told Merrah did. I sent him home, but we've added a few more patients."

"Some good news, at least, with the man who improved. If we get them early, we have a chance. Even if they're a higher risk. I'll take whatever I can get as far as hope." A hard knot of tension formed between Ghost's shoulders. "Do you have enough supplies? If you're low, ask Gerry if he can trade for more. And tell him to bring the liver loaf to the warehouse. If I'm not there to remind him to eat, it'll only go to waste."

Natali chuckled. "He growls so nicely when prodded, Gerry does. He says he's eating. He brought us the better part of a runner already, and he's been here to help all day and into the night. We have a great many volunteers. You have a strong community here."

"How fares the elder?" Ghost asked. "I'm hoping he gets through this and recovers."

"He's here. He's not getting worse, which is all I can say for now. Not as good as getting better. But so far, he's holding on." Natali paused again. "Your Gerry wants me to tell you he loves you. And he wants you to come home as quickly as you can."

Ghost sighed. "Please tell Gerry I love him, more than I know how to say. I need to look for the Witch and see if I can help her. The more I learn, the more important finding her becomes. Tell him I will come home. And I will. I won't let anything stop me." He paused and added, "I found some healers' supplies. Things I've only ever read about. If nothing else, I might be able to use some of this to help the worst cases. I'll see what I can figure out as I'm traveling. There's not much else to do. But I have to go on."

"I understand. Seeker guide you, brother. I'll do what I can for the afflicted. Your infusions work if we can get the patients early enough in the illness. The trick is getting stubborn people to admit they're sick. But Merrah and Mai help to convince them, and I appreciate their dedication. Your Gerry worked hard to get the worst cases here, and Conn is back too." Natali's smile came through clearly in her gentle sending.

"Thank you for being there for the village, sister. And thank Gerry for being there for them too. I didn't want to leave in the middle of this epidemic, but if I can do more by finding the Witch, I need to take that path. I'm following where the Seeker leads me." Ghost sighed. "Tell Gerry I wish he was here because he'd love this. He really would. One day, if I'm allowed, I want to take him on a journey. Tell him I love him and to take care of himself."

"He says he loves you, and he'll do his best. He says he misses you, and the bed is too big." Natali added, "Be well, witchbrother."

Natali's witchmark faded, and Ghost leaned back against the pillows, resting for a moment before he began to visualize the Witch's red triskele. Perhaps she was listening, or perhaps she would sense him as he got closer. Ghost did not know, but either way, he was determined to find the Witch and a cure for his village. He would trust Gerry and Natali to deal with the sick until he could get back home.

Chapter Twelve

GHOST FOCUSED ON the red triskele until his eyes nearly crossed and his head ached. He did not want to waste the healers' supplies he had found on something so minor, and he had no idea how to use Menu to make a tea for himself. Lying down and closing his eyes for a while, until he could no longer feel the throbbing, helped.

The red dot on the map continued along the line, and the slow progress was reassuring. The lighting from the other panels changed as the day wore on, the way Ghost supposed natural sunlight would change direction and intensity. The panels were nothing like having real windows, but it was a way to measure time. He dug in his leather pouch and found the box that held his pen and a small bottle of ink. He opened his formulary to the blank sheets at the back and took a careful inventory of the items he had found in the healers' container.

Ghost was absorbed in his task, and he only paused when his stomach growled loud enough to startle him. Menu supplied a bean stew served over rice. The stew was spicy and reminded Ghost of Gerry's dislike of overly savory foods, which made him miss Gerry even more.

Thinking of Gerry made Ghost's throat tighten. Speaking through Natali had been frustrating. He'd wanted to tell Gerry so many things, but it was awkward asking the sweet-voiced witch to repeat them. The words were too intimate, and the emotions too raw. No, those were things he needed to say to Gerry when he returned home.

Reading some of Information's content was next on Ghost's list. He hoped to find any scraps of information that might help him. Unlike the godsmen, he considered ignorance a bigger fault than remembering the ancient words. He did think the cities, as the Witch had explained them, were overwhelming, and he could not imagine living in proximity to so very many people. All those voices, all at once, would have been an unbearable cacophony. Still, the bits and pieces gleaned from the ruins had made a difference. The gods' light, the Seeker's kiss, even the witchglass. These had all been used to save lives. How much more were those long-dead city dwellers capable of, if a few remnants could accomplish so much?

Ghost became engrossed in his reading, so much so, he missed the early tugging on his spiral heralding contact. He hurried over to the bench to dig out his scrying mirror and settled on the bed again. Ghost opened himself up to the contact and waited patiently until the mirror clouded. A symbol formed, an emerald leaf, signaling Beccah of the East Marches.

"Ghost, my brother, where are you?" Beccah asked without any preamble. "A terrible commotion has arisen among some of the sisterhood, and I'm taking shelter with Kerree for a time. Are you safe?"

"I'm not sure if 'safe' is the word I'd use," Ghost replied, puzzled by Beccah's designation of him as her brother, since she was part of Sri's group. "I'm on my way to the Northlands. I have reason to think a solution is there."

"You must go quickly. Very quickly. Do you know of the faster ways we travel?" Beccah spoke with care, even though no one else was in the contact to hear her mental voice.

"Yes." Ghost paused. "Why are you so concerned? And why the urgency?"

Beccah's voice was tense. "I spoke with Tal of the West Reaches, and she will contact you herself. Now I need to leave and find shelter from the coming storms. Safe harbor, little brother."

Beccah cut the contact, and Ghost winced at the abrupt closure. "I wish they wouldn't end the link so fast," he muttered. "It hurts every single time." He shook his head, trying to clear the pain, but it did little good.

Ghost fell back onto the pile of pillows, not much compensation for the emptiness of his bed. He missed Gerry with such intensity the longing manifested as physical pain. He had changed since meeting Gerry. He was a furtive little shadow back then, trying to hide behind the Witch, but Gerry had wanted him anyway. Now Ghost longed for his mate. He never wanted to go back to being alone, and despite the way they had parted, Ghost knew they could mend their relationship. He would make sure they did.

A new tug at his spiral startled him, and Ghost reached for his mirror again, wondering if Beccah had thought of something else. He didn't bother to mask his headache, annoyed at her for ending the contact as she had. The symbol forming in his mirror was elaborate knotwork in fierce ruby red, however.

"Ghost? Is this my brother, the witch called Ghost?" The voice was tentative, but the harsh accent marked the contact as being a Wester.

"I'm Ghost," he responded, doing his best to ignore the headache. "You're Tal? I was told you would contact me, sister."

"I can offer little, I fear, beyond urging you to go to the Northlands with all haste. Find the Witch who mentored you. She has the solution. I did what I could. I got him away from here, and now I need to leave myself. Trust the Witch.

The rest of us are weaker than she is." Tal's voice wavered. "I must go, brother witch."

Tal eased out of the contact before Ghost could respond, leaving him more puzzled and more afraid than ever. He put the scrying mirror away and rubbed his temples with his fingers.

"HE REALLY SAID so? Twice?" Gerry knew he had to sound like an idiot, and Natali's amusement did not help.

"Your Ghost loves you, and yes, he said so twice." Natali shook her head. "What a pity you're not a witch, or he could tell you himself. He loves you. He wants you to take care of yourself. He will be home as soon as he can. And he misses you as much as you miss him. I hear the longing in both your voices."

"You didn't tell him about the pregnant dam," Gerry said. He winced at the undertone of accusation in his voice. "I didn't mean to sound so harsh. But shouldn't he know right away, if the plague is affecting a new group?"

"He already knew about her. He chalked her door himself. Ghost worries whether he's done the right thing in leaving, but he can't return without the answers he's seeking." Natali made a shooing gesture at Gerry. "Now, get out of my way. I have patients to tend to, and your Ghost won't thank me if I fail him."

Gerry moved aside and watched Natali make her rounds from bed to bed. She asked the elderly and the very young to stay. The others were treated and sent home with packets of the infusion and Ghost's instructions in the careful pictographs they would understand. The elder of the village was eating again and holding down his food. Gerry wished Ghost was there to see these small victories.

The babes, though, tore at Gerry's heart the most. He saw the grief in Natali's eyes. They all mourned for those helpless mites; Mai, Merrah, and even Conn. Listening to the cries of the babes grow weaker as the sobs of the dams grew louder was more than Gerry could handle. He needed to be out in the fresh air and away from the misery. He wanted Ghost to be there so he could tell Ghost he had been wrong one more time. Gerry walked along the edge of the market, his strides longer and longer until he was all but running. He stopped when he reached Mother's yard.

Mother was out in the back, wrapping a smoked runner haunch. He straightened up as Gerry strode into the yard, leading Gerry into the house without a word. He pointed Gerry to the table near the hearth and rummaged in a cabinet.

"How can she stand the crying? How does Ghost stand it?" Gerry buried his fingers in his hair, his elbows on the table as he slumped forward.

"The same way my dam stood it. Dealing with their suffering is part of the trade as a healer." Mother put a small cup in front of Gerry and poured something pungent from a glass bottle into the cup. "This might help. Then again, maybe not. But it won't hurt."

Gerry watched as Mother poured some into a second cup. "What is this?" In all the years he had lived with Mother, he had never seen the bottle or the drink it held.

Mother smiled. "It's called metheglin. A spicy aged mead. Stronger than what you'd find in the mead house."

Gerry picked up the cup and took a swallow. The flavor was much different than what he was expecting. The taste was richer, sharp with ginger and clove. The metheglin warmed him as it slid down his throat. He set the cup down with care.

Mother chuckled and drank his cup down in a single draught. "Healers need to learn to let go. Just as hunters must learn to kill clean. Letting a runner get away with a fatal wound is cruel. Hunting is not about the runners suffering. It's the same for a witch."

Gerry sighed and turned the cup in a slow circle. "Natali said the patient has to be able to understand and accept or refuse the tincture. So, the babes can't be helped. I don't know how she can stay there and watch. The dams know, and they're as helpless." He picked up the cup and finished the drink. "I was so wrong to even think I could judge Ghost."

"You'll tell him when he comes home." Mother offered the bottle, but Gerry waved it away. "He will come home. Believe in him. Witches have their own ways and secrets. They walk in places where we wouldn't go willingly. For all you feel the need to protect him, Ghost is capable and clever."

Gerry managed a smile. "He's both those things and more. He's so damned single-minded sometimes. He doesn't give up. He sat up nights reading his formulary until I all but dragged him to bed. Otherwise, he'd have gone to see his patients with no sleep, no breakfast, no anything. But he's passionate about being a witch. You should have seen him tell Moran off and face the elders. I was so proud of him."

"You've been proud of him since you first took him as your dependent. It's a rare witch who's a dependent, you know. My dam was the alpha of our family, and my sire her dependent," Mother said. "He makes you proudest when he's being a witch and standing on his own. Have you told him?"

Gerry swallowed hard. "The words don't come easy. My tongue mangles what I want to say. To say I love him seems inadequate."

"You'll find a way, and he'll forgive you. It will all work out." Mother stood and walked out of the room, leaving Gerry alone with the metheglin and his misery.

GHOST READ MORE of the entries from Information while the carriage hurtled north. The red dot moved closer to the end point, and Ghost judged he would arrive at the station well before high sun tomorrow. Ghost yawned and found himself ridiculously tired from doing nothing, far more tired than dealing with the sick would have left him.

Finally, Ghost closed Information and put away his formulary and pen. The bed was cool, and he took a moment to shift the pillows around and give himself the illusion of being home. He did not bother to lower the lighting in the carriage. Darkness would not have helped him relax, and he felt safer when he could see.

The carriage lurched, and Ghost woke as he was jostled in his nest of pillows. The lighting grew dim, the panels as black as could be. He wondered if the carriage had not been fed enough, or maybe the path the carriage followed was blocked or damaged. Another lurch jolted him, stronger than before, and a high-pitched whine filled his ears briefly. The carriage settled back down and the lighting grew brighter again, but Ghost could not relax. He huddled back under the blankets until he grew too restless.

Ghost climbed out of the bed and called up the map. The red dot had veered off the line, but the position was far closer to the end point than he had expected. He did not want to know how the new path had been implemented.

Ghost cleaned the cabin and checked his pouches. He barely noticed the porridge he ate for breakfast, too busy watching the red dot close on the station.

The carriage hummed and slowed down. Ghost's stomach fluttered, and he reached for the water skin to take a drink. The lighting dimmed for a moment, and a panel shifted to display a message.

"Arrival at terminal station eight imminent," Ghost read aloud. "Prepare to disembark." He frowned as he tried to decide what "disembark" could mean. He grabbed his pouches and water skin and slung his cloak over his shoulders. The carriage came to a halt and the door slid open.

"Welcome to terminal station eight." Ghost heard the same voice from the station back in the Heartlands. He stepped through the door with alacrity, not willing to take any chances with this "disembark" thing.

Frost rimed the walls of the station, and Ghost's boots crunched over the thin crust of ice covering the floor. He drew his cloak tighter around him. The lights flickered in places, but most of this station remained shadowed and dim.

Information had been unable to provide any reliable clues about the Northlands. Too much had changed since the entries had been written. The map still showed the East Marches as solid land, after all, and Ghost knew they were nothing but a jumble of islands. But the lack of data meant he had no idea what would await him outside the station. He did not know if a Norther equivalent to sind or an even bigger predator lurked in the frozen wastes. Not as though it would matter, if Ghost was being honest with himself. He needed to find the Witch and her potential vaccine, and he would face whatever waited out there.

Because the voice of this station was the same, Ghost took a chance in assuming the design of the station would be similar as well. He guessed he was in a substation and needed to find his way to the main station to locate an exit. He proceeded with caution, listening to the echo of his steps as he entered the cavern of the main station, the openings of other substations black maws on the icy walls.

Ghost marveled at the spines of ice hanging from the ceiling. They were as deadly as they were beautiful should they fall, however, and he stayed as close to the wall as possible while crossing the main station. The exit would be across from the substations, if the pattern held true. If not, hugging the walls would lead him to an exit sooner or later.

Despite the warmth of his cloak, Ghost registered a chill as he made his careful way around the perimeter of the room. He almost missed the corridor to the exit, so absorbed was he in watching the faint light playing on the icicles above. A puff of colder air alerted him, and he turned to peer into the corridor.

The bitter cold must have broken the lights, because the corridor was not lit at all. Ghost reached out to touch the wall, his fingers skimming the frigid surface, and he shivered at even such a slight contact. He stopped to grope in his pouch for the leather mitts Gerry had made to match his cloak, lined with the thinner belly fur of the sind.

The time needed to transit the station seemed greater here, but at long last, his foot bumped the first step. Climbing upward in total darkness was disconcerting, and Ghost strained to hear any sounds. He could smell nothing beyond the sharp bite of the frigid air that grew colder as Ghost climbed, and the chill penetrated his boots. The stairs took longer to navigate than in the first station, although it could have been the darkness altering his perceptions.

Ghost discovered the door by walking into it. His mitt brushed over a raised area, and a groaning sound accompanied a dazzling line of light as the door opened. Icy crystals sparkled in the gust of air that blew inward.

His first impression was whiteness. Unrelieved, stark whiteness. Ghost's eyes teared as the light flooded them after the trek through the darkness of the corridor. He ducked his head, tugging his hood farther forward to shield his eyes, one mitted hand shading them as the tears froze to his lashes.

"Oh, Seeker," Ghost murmured. He took a few faltering steps, not wanting to remain in the door in case it closed again. He had never felt such biting cold, and he pulled his cloak tightly around himself, grateful for the thick leathers he wore under the heavy fur. He let his eyes adjust to the brightness, blinking a few times to clear away the bits of ice from his lashes.

At least the wind was slight. He had enough to do just trying to breathe without his lungs aching. He remembered a rare, bitter-cold winter in his youth, when the Witch had told him to breathe through his nose to warm the air. He tried her advice now, and the air was not so biting when it reached his lungs.

Ghost's heart sank when he took in the landscape, if it could be called such. The snow was pristine, the surface unmarred by so much as a footprint, and the ice shone like glass. Even the sky was white, with sullen streaks of pale gray hinting at heavier weather on the horizon.

Ghost pushed past his worries and concerns. He sought the trace of the Witch in his witchmark and focused all his will, but her presence remained elusive.

"Seeker, Witch, stop blocking me," Ghost muttered. Standing still was an effort in this cold, and he shivered. "I need to find shelter."

Ghost did not suppose this station would be anywhere closer to a village than the station where he had begun his journey. The ancient places were shunned by most sane people, witches and rangers being less sane than most. He supposed Northers were by definition at least as crazy as witches. Living in such a stark and unforgiving place was surely insane. He began to walk in the direction most likely to lead away from the station, finding a vague sort of path in the unbroken white of the landscape.

As he walked, Ghost noticed he was getting a stronger sense of the Witch's presence. A subtle increase, but enough to register. He let the faint link guide him as he searched for the stones with the witchmarks he remembered from his vision. But if they were there, the snow and ice had covered them.

The snow got heavier as Ghost walked along, but he did not pay any attention at first. In another moon or so, there would be snow in the Heartlands as well, and the snowfall did not trigger an alarm in Ghost right away. When he realized he could not see more than an arm's length in front of himself, he grew concerned. The wind was rising, and the icy flakes blew under his hood to sting his face. He stumbled over something uneven beneath his feet. Wandering in a storm was far too dangerous. Shelter was now an urgent necessity.

From somewhere long forgotten, Ghost remembered reading about digging a hole in the snow and using the hollow as a way to hold in the heat. Gerry said sind did the same thing. Gerry had told him you would see the small hole in a mound of snow, and if you listened, you could hear the sind breathing and see little puffs of fog rising from the hole. When you stopped seeing the puffs, you had to worry, because the sind was awake and had heard you.

The idea of being some predator's dinner was unappealing, but so was freezing to death. Ghost could barely feel his feet, and the snow was getting heavier by the moment. He stumbled again, putting out his hand to lean on the rock face he had been walking beside. His hand slid off and went past the face almost the length of his arm before making contact with more rock.

"A recess," Ghost muttered to himself. "This can work."

Ghost stepped into the indentation in the rock face, nodding in satisfaction when the angle deflected the wind. He crouched down, trying to build up a wall of snow to block off the recess as much as possible. His mitts made him clumsy, and the wind pushed at his construction, but he persevered until he had built up the snow as high as his chest.

Ghost could still sense the Witch's presence, and he did his best to reach out along the thread to provoke contact. She remained silent, but the sense of her was stronger than ever. He recalled the cloak of white fur she wore in his vision. She felt the same now, both welcoming and unfamiliar at the same time. He drew his own cloak around him a little tighter, the hood falling over his eyes for a moment as he settled in to wait out the snow.

Crouched down in his impromptu shelter, Ghost felt fatigue creeping over him. All he wanted was to rest for a while, even though he knew it was far too dangerous to sleep. He would reach out to the Witch and use the effort to keep himself alert. And after he had rested, he would see if the snow had eased and he could continue onward.

The fur around Ghost's face was warm and soft, and he leaned his head to one side, resting against the ice-rimed rock. He let his eyes close, and the dark was soothing after looking at endless white. Ghost's head ached from the cold.

If Gerry had been there, Ghost could have asked him for something hot and soothing, but not hemp. Sleep was bad, and he might not see Gerry if he slept. A voice agreed, but not Gerry, though. Gerry's voice was deeper and ran along Ghost's spine to settle in his belly, warming him from the inside out. The Witch had spoken, and he nodded, his eyes closing tightly as his breathing evened out and slowed.

Chapter Thirteen

WARM. WARM, STRONG arms surrounded him. Ghost smiled and moved closer, burying his face in the hard muscle of a shoulder. He knew he needed to get up to tend to his patients, but he was still so tired. He nuzzled deeper into the shoulder that was...clearly not Gerry's.

"The little one wakes." A deep, rumbling voice pierced his fog of sleep.

Ghost shoved hard against the arms holding him. He wriggled free and sat up, a door closing somewhere behind him. "Let go of me," he growled. He was wide awake now, and his heart pounded against his ribs.

The man belonging to the arms was bare-chested, as was Ghost, to his chagrin. He was relieved to see he still wore his breeches, though relief did not stop him from glaring at the man in the bed with him.

"You're fierce, little one. This is good to see. It means you are not too soft, like the rest of the outlanders from down below." The man sat up as well. His long white hair was bound back in many braids, each one tipped with a bead carved from the red wood of the South. An intricate black tattoo covered both his arms. The man's blue eyes watched Ghost with undisguised amusement. "You have jewels in your head, little one. Did the woman decorate you so?"

"What woman?" Ghost retorted, watching the man for any untoward movement. "Are you talking about the Witch? Is she here?"

"Outlanders do not ask. They listen. And answer." The man's voice dropped to a warning snarl. "Hair and eyes do not make you one of us, little one. Do not presume you have a place here."

"I don't want a place here," Ghost snapped. "I want to talk to the Witch. She may have the solution I need. The people of my village await my return."

A large, calloused hand clapped Ghost's shoulder as the man barked out a laugh. "There was not a single question in all your words. This is good to know. You are both fierce and can listen."

Ghost snorted, moving out from under the hand and off the bed, the central feature of the room. The walls were timber, broad planks lacquered to a glossy shine. White hide curtains closed off a small window. Below the window was a carved wooden chest with a rounded lid, painted as elaborately as the man's tattooed arms. He looked around for the rest of his clothing. "Makes one of us," he muttered, not looking up. He tried to ignore the laughter from the bed as he found his thick linen shirt and heavy leather tunic tossed in a corner.

Getting dressed made Ghost feel much better, and finding his tall boots more so. He looked around for a place to sit to put them on, but there was just the large bed with the muscular Norther in it, and Ghost had no intentions of getting close to the man again. He sat on the floor and tugged the first boot over his foot.

"Will you talk about the stones?" the big man asked, crossing thick arms over his broad, muscled chest.

"Only if you tell me why I was in bed with you." Ghost stood, peering around the room to see if he could spot his pouches and his beautiful cloak. If this oaf of a Norther had taken his cloak, Ghost was going to figure out a way to inflict a proper curse on the bastard.

"That earns you my name. Not many people would bargain with me. I am Njall, son of Falkor. Do you have a name, little one?" The man watched Ghost with open amusement.

"I am Ghost, mate of Gerry, witch to my village." Ghost eyed Njall. "I'm still waiting for my answer."

"You were found in the snow, half-frozen and asleep, little Ghost. You tried to make a shelter, which was wise, but you slept before you were done. Not so wise." Njall shrugged. "Your pretty cloak marked you as an outlander almost as much as the unfinished shelter. Now, my answer?"

"I'm not sure what woman you mean," Ghost replied, not looking away from Njall. "But if you mean a woman with three joined spirals in red on her forehead, then yes. She gave me my witchmark." He crossed his own arms over his chest. "She is who I came to find."

"The woman with the triskele, yes. She is an outlander, but she is fierce as well. She came to speak with Falkor, and when I mistook her for a thrall, a serving woman, she slapped me." Njall laughed his rumbling laugh. "I like her, although she is too old to give me sons. She had a boy with her, though."

This reminded Ghost of his own missing items. "I'd like my cloak back. And my pouches. The cloak was a gift from my mate. He made it with his own hands. The pouches hold my healers' supplies, and I need those for my people."

"You will get your items back, little Ghost. We are not savages, to steal from guests in the halls of our clanhold." Njall threw back the thick quilts, naked as the day he had been birthed. He grinned at Ghost with abundant cheer, and Ghost growled and turned away.

"So, tell me, why did you come to find your woman with the triskele? I am told she calls herself Witch. A name as well as a title?" Njall rustled about, and Ghost risked turning back, to see Njall fastening woven breeches.

"The Witch contacted me to tell me she might have information about an illness ravaging my village. I was her apprentice and took her place when she moved on." Ghost watched Njall, the Norther graceful for such a large man as he pulled a linen tunic over his head. "This malady is not a typical illness, and witches commonly ask each other for aid and information when a crisis occurs, such as an epidemic."

"Do your people still hide from books, little Ghost? Do the shamans speak against the old knowledge?" Njall pulled on boots and gestured for Ghost to follow him into a well-lit hallway walled in whitewashed timber.

Ghost tried to puzzle out the word Njall had used. "We don't have shamans," he said. "I don't know what they do."

"Speak to the gods, or so they say," Njall said with a shrug. "More often, they meddle in matters not of their concern."

"Godsmen," Ghost said, nodding in understanding. "Yes, the godsmen still say the old learning is what brought down the world once. They only tolerate the witchsisters because we can use some of the old relics to heal."

"Witchsisters, is it? When I held you close to warm you, I was quite sure it was not a girl's desire that pressed against my leg, little Ghost." Njall rumbled a laugh as Ghost glared at him. "I jest with you. Well, not so much, since you did press against me, but the reaction was simply what a man's body will do and not the heat of desire. I am not such a savage as to mistake the two."

"I never said you were a savage," Ghost countered. "And I'm the first male admitted to the ranks of the witchsisters in many generations. I'm not exactly popular with all of the sisterhood, but I passed their tests and took the vows. I suppose if you don't have witches, your shamans heal you, then."

"Yes and no." Njall opened a carved door painted in shades of blue and gestured for Ghost to enter. "We have healers of our own, both men and women who are called to such service under the guidance of the shamans. They deal with issues of the body, and the shamans deal with the concerns of the soul. But our gods are not your soft outlander gods, little Ghost. Our gods will eat your liver raw, and this is only if they like you."

Ghost's retort died on his lips as he took in the sight before him. Books. Walls lined with them. Tables and benches littered with careless stacks. Njall's chuckle propelled Ghost farther into the room.

"When the cities fell, little Ghost, our people decided someone would have to preserve the knowledge. Your frightened godsmen called the collapse the wrath of the gods. They urged your people to turn their backs on the learning that had made life too easy. They were half right." Njall walked past Ghost to pick up a book, turning the tome over in his large hands. "Life had gotten too soft, but such lassitude was not the fault of the learning. The leaders wanted sheep. Fat, comfortable sheep, who would not bleat too loud as long as they had good grazing. But these are matters best left to others. Falkor leads our clan. I am only a simple warrior, and I prefer to read the words of warriors past."

"You read?" Ghost marveled at the books, his fingers itching with the desire to touch them.

"Then the tales are true? The outlanders do not teach their people to read?" Njall sounded almost disgusted.

Ghost pulled his attention from the books to look at Njall. "Witches read. So do the rangers who travel between lands and scavenge the ruins." Ghost dared to pick up a book, running his fingers over the cover with reverence before opening it. "The rest of the people use pictographs and tally marks. But even among the witchsisters and the rangers, most read what they have to. I like to read. I had a little hiding place in a ruin near the Witch's house. I had my books there and a candle to read by."

"So, this outlander woman was your mother?" Njall asked.

"No. She raised me, but she wasn't my dam." Ghost looked up from his book. "She told me she found me, and she didn't know where my dam was, or my sire. She never said where she found me, though. I never really asked. I was happy enough with her."

"And no one remarked on how you look? Are there many who look like you in your soft little village?" Njall leaned against a stout table strewn with books.

Ghost returned the book he was holding to the shelf. "I'd like to know why you're asking all this. Call me suspicious, but I'm not entirely comfortable with answering any more questions." He folded his arms over his chest and frowned up at the warrior, his heart beating a little faster. Njall could no doubt snap him in two, but Ghost was growing irritated at the questioning, since he had been told he could not ask questions of his own.

"Better me asking than Bruadar," Njall replied, the cryptic reference unsettling. "Falkor wishes to know, and I serve my father in this. You look like one of us, but it is rare one of our people would lose a child and not seek to find what is lost. The rangers who serve the slavers raid the borders, and we have lost a few to them, but the woman is no slaver. So, who left you to be found by her, and why? These are the questions Falkor asks. I must assume you have no answers, which is a pity because she is not inclined to answer herself. Perhaps you can persuade her."

"If you hurt her, I'll kill you." Ghost glared at Njall. "I'm not persuading the Witch to tell you anything. And if you think threatening me will get you anywhere, think again."

"Hush, little Ghost," Njall said, his irritating look of amusement back. "No one has hurt the outlander woman. She is also a guest in our halls. But she did not come alone, as I have said, and the boy she brought with her is one of our people, as are you. So, you can see why Falkor would have questions. Who is this Witch who seeks out and rescues our lost children?"

Ghost growled under his breath, but he found himself wondering the same thing. "She's not an enemy," he said at last. "So, take me to her."

"There is no need. I have already sent for her." Njall gave Ghost a broad smile. "We will meet in the food hall. We will break bread together and enlighten each other. But first, little Ghost, choose a book or two for yourself, as compensation for my jesting with you. What interests you most?"

"Books about healing," Ghost said. "If you have books about medicines or herbal remedies, I'd be grateful."

Njall snorted, clapping one large hand onto Ghost's shoulder, and Ghost did his best not to stagger. He felt as though he had been patted with a runner haunch.

"I did not mean that sort of book, little Ghost. I do not think Falkor will object to sharing one or two educational books, but what would amuse you, and occupy you on those long, cool nights you think are winter?" Njall reached for a book with a red leather cover. "This is a book of small stories about fantastical creatures and strange worlds. Who knows? Perhaps they were even real once."

Njall placed the red leather book in Ghost's hands. "And this one is an adventure on the oceans of the world. Very stirring." Njall dropped the second book into Ghost's hands, and quirked an eyebrow at him. "Or do you like stories about magic and mystery? Evil deeds and swift justice? Love lost and found again?"

Ghost knew he must look like a wide-eyed child at a festival for the first time. This many books, and he had no idea what he wanted to read, just for himself. Njall was a whirlwind, pulling out book after book with casual familiarity, and Ghost could not help blurting out, "Have you read all these books?"

Njall stopped. "Most of them. I do not care for books about love. I am a warrior and not a skald." He smiled when Ghost raised his eyebrows at the unfamiliar term. "A singer of epic songs. But I must read a book describing a great battle if I find one. I cannot resist. You look so surprised, little Ghost. Have I not told you? We are not savages."

"No, you're not," Ghost replied. "Then if I can name what I want, I want the book of small stories and one with magic." He felt his heart beat a little harder as he waited to be rebuffed.

"Wise choices," Njall said, taking back the books Ghost had not wanted, leaving him holding the red leather book and another bound in dark brown cloth. He paused and grabbed a third book. "Herbs and plants, and their uses. For the sake of your village. These are the gift of Njall. What Falkor gives will come from his own hand."

"I wonder about the custom for guests, if a return gift is polite or even expected?" Ghost glanced up at Njall. He did not have a great deal he could offer as a gift, but he had a few attractive arm rings in worked copper. The jewelry would never fit Njall, but Njall could give them to someone. Maybe a woman or a child. Ghost would have nothing for Falkor, though.

Njall opened the door to the hallway again. "Honesty is a gift I prize, and I think you have been honest with me, little Ghost. Falkor will expect answers, and he may not enjoy your fierce words as much as I do."

THE SAVORY FRAGRANCE of roasting meat and spices filled the food hall and lured Ghost into the room. Njall led the way through the rows of long wooden tables, the tops scrubbed pale. The benches flanking each table were padded, to Ghost's surprise. Young men and women moved through the rows of tables, offering food and pouring drinks from large copper pitchers.

Ghost's stomach grumbled in response to the rich aromas, and Njall looked over his shoulder in frank amusement. Njall came to a stop close to the front of the room, at a table placed perpendicular to a low platform. He gestured for Ghost to take a seat and lowered himself next to Ghost.

"The table in front of us is where Falkor dines. I sit at his feet with his most trusted warriors and his other sons." Njall smiled at the young woman who approached with a laden tray. A second woman filled Njall's mug with a small amount of mead topped by hot water. Njall waved her to give Ghost the same drink.

"Do not drink too much mead this early in the day, little Ghost. Falkor will want to speak to you." Njall turned to the women. "Four plates and two more mugs. I expect two more guests this morning."

Njall turned back to Ghost. "This meat is bjarrn. It is a little strong to the taste, but good when cooked like this."

In front of Ghost, the woman set a plate laden with boiled eggs, warm bread, and meat in rich gravy. Ghost's stomach grumbled again, and he heard a familiar dry voice from behind him.

"You took your time, little one."

Ghost turned on the bench so fast that he nearly tumbled to the floor. Only Njall's large hand in the small of his back kept him on the bench. His mouth opened and closed again with a sharp snap as he stared in frank amazement.

If not for her voice, he would not have recognized the Witch at first glance. The greasy-haired hag in rusty black homespun was gone. The Witch's hair was clean and soft, pulled back into a single silver braid held with a twisted leather cord. She wore a long shift in soft wool the color of a summer sky, and a gold torc rested atop her collarbones. The red triskele stood out against her pale skin, and her dark eyes were as sharp as ever.

The boy with her was another matter. He was a Norther, his hair as white as Njall's, pulled back to hold it off his face. He wore a simple linen tunic and woven breeches like Njall, and there the resemblance ended. The boy looked at the Witch for instruction and snuck a peek at Ghost from under thick lashes once she guided him to his seat beside her. Ghost returned the inquisitive glance openly. The boy looked to be no more than nine or ten years of age, far too thin and pale for Ghost's liking, and he was clearly terrified.

"I'd have been here faster if you'd bothered to tell me about the witchpaths," Ghost replied. "A little practical advice on the local climate wouldn't have hurt, either."

Njall waited for the Witch to get settled, but Ghost noticed Njall did not wait for the boy before beginning to eat. The boy sat and stared at his plate until the Witch touched his arm. "Eat, child. A good wind would blow you over."

The words were familiar enough to make Ghost give the Witch a sharp look. He took a sip of the watered mead while he gathered his scattered thoughts. The Witch had used the same tone with him when he was young. The flash of resentment he felt surprised him.

"This is Egill," the Witch said. "I'm told we're all supposed to meet with Falkor later this morning. He leads this clan, and he's very curious about my motives for being here. Patience, little one, is not one of Falkor's strongest traits. If you'd been much later, I'd have been getting a bit uncomfortable."

"Why?" Ghost looked up from his plate. The hint of temper in the Witch's tone made him feel uneasy. "I came here with questions of my own, although I'm told outlanders aren't supposed to ask anything. I'm pretty sure I won't have the answers to Falkor's questions." He looked at Njall, who shrugged one broad shoulder and returned to eating.

The Witch smiled, but Ghost was sure her dark eyes held no humor at all.

"I have answers Falkor wants, but I won't give him any satisfaction until I hear what's going on from you." The Witch sipped her watered mead and gestured for more water. "Falkor's shaman, Bruadar, has been kind enough to teach me about some of the healing techniques used here. Plants and herbs grown only in this locale. It's fascinating."

Ghost heard the unspoken warning in the Witch's words. She considered Bruadar a danger, more so than Falkor. Njall had implied as much himself. These Norther shamans had teeth, unlike the godsmen of the Heartlands. Ghost took a bite of the meat and chewed, irritated by whatever game was being played here.

"Is there any way to get word from home? I'd like to see how the village is doing." Ghost gave Njall a stern look as he spoke. "I also want to talk to my mate and let him know I'm all right. I'd do it myself, but I don't seem to have my pouch."

Njall sat back, pushing his empty plate away. "How did you know to find your Witch here, little Ghost?"

"We're back to this." Ghost glared at the warrior without flinching. "I'm a witch, and our ways are our own. And this is about all you're getting until someone tells me what's going on here. I have profoundly sick people whose lives depend on me, and all I want is some help curing them. The rest doesn't matter to me."

"Not completely housebroken," the Witch muttered.

Egill went very still, his spoon halfway to his mouth. His eyes remained fixed on his plate, and he flinched when the Witch touched his shoulder.

"Be easy, child. Ghost has learned to growl, it seems. No one will punish you for his words. This is not the West Reaches." The Witch looked over at Njall, and Ghost noted the defiant lift of her chin.

"Do not look at me so, woman." Njall's voice was heavy. "I will not waste good breath asking questions you will not answer. I have no means to compel you, although I am not sure Falkor or Bruadar will have an easier time of it. Finish your meal, and we will see."

Chapter Fourteen

GHOST AND THE Witch followed Njall as he strode through the maze of timber-walled hallways that comprised the clanhold. Ghost clutched the books Njall had given him to his chest as he gazed up at the heads of strange beasts mounted on the walls of a large room. A white-furred specimen with a long muzzle and vicious fangs looked as though it could have taken a man's arm off with a casual snap.

"He is a bjarrn. He was a canny old one, this one, and put up quite the fight. Falkor had the honor of the kill." Njall grinned at Ghost, and Ghost gave the head a last baleful look before turning away.

They passed through another hallway and stopped in front of a large door made from the red wood of the South. Elaborate reliefs covered the door, and Ghost was surprised to see many of the markings he recognized as witchmarks among the carvings. He dared to glance over at the Witch, and he met her eyes with a blast of pure apprehension. His blood ran cold as the stones from his vision rose up in his mind's eye.

Njall looked over at Ghost, his expression amused. "We do trade with outlanders, you know. They covet our jewels and the white furs of our little viksin, or the thick hides of the elkkur. Your pretty jewels might have come from our mountains, little Ghost. Some outlanders request the teeth of the bjarrn, but those are not given without much thought.

The shamans say the teeth hold power. And for all I know, they might even be right."

Njall opened the door to reveal a large man sitting atop a dais in a high-backed chair carved with the same intricacy as the door. A slightly smaller man in dark robes stood at the right hand of the seated man.

The man on the dais resembled Njall, but his face bore the weathering of age. He wore a tunic embroidered in vivid colors and a cloak of white fur, similar to the one the Witch had worn in Ghost's vision. A thick gold torc with ends of polished ruby circled his neck. Based on the resemblance, the man had to be Falkor, Njall's father and the leader of the clan. The man behind the chair was therefore Bruadar, the shaman.

Ghost studied Bruadar with careful interest. Unlike Njall or Falkor, Bruadar had eyes as dark as the Witch's. He had not mastered the Witch's ability to hide behind an expressionless face, though. He frowned as he watched Njall escort the small group into the room. Bruadar's eyes never left the Witch and Egill. He spared less than a glance for Ghost.

"As you desired, Falkor, I have brought the outlander woman and the two of our blood here to speak with you. This one is called Ghost." Njall motioned for Ghost to stand alongside the Witch and Egill. "The small one is called Egill." Njall did not bow or show any signs of subservience, and he ignored Bruadar entirely as he took up a position behind Ghost.

"Have they shared what they know, Njall, son of Falkor, or have you failed in this task?" Bruadar's voice was harsh and raspy, and his dark eyes shifted to Njall.

Njall chuckled. "I am no skald to be telling stories. If there is something you want to know, ask them, shaman. I serve my father, not the gods." He dropped one large hand onto Ghost's shoulder. Whether the gesture was a warning or support, Ghost could not say.

"Be still, the both of you." Falkor's voice was as deep a rumble as Njall's voice. "This is my hall. I will ask what needs to be asked." He turned his faded blue eyes to Ghost. "How did you come to be here? Your manner of dress and the mark on your head show you to be an outlander. Yet the passes by which your kind travel are closed by the autumn snows."

Ghost met Falkor's eyes without flinching. He heard a small whisper in the back of his mind, almost like speaking to the witchsisters. It was not the Witch, though, nor was it a voice he recognized. The tone was shy, but the words were sharp. *Bruadar doesn't know about the carriages, and you shouldn't tell him.*

Ghost hoped he was as expressionless as the Witch as he answered Falkor. "The witches have their own ways."

"And what are those ways?" Falkor asked.

Ghost shook his head. "You haven't taken the vows. I won't speak of witchsister business with an outsider."

"My business is to ensure the safety of my clan," Falkor retorted. "And yet I am confronted with unexpected guests in a season when none travel this way. Two of those guests look to be Norther born. A puzzling thing because we do not let our children wander, to be taken up by outlanders and raised as strangers. Should I fear for my children and the children of my people? This woman tells me no, but I find no solace in her assurances."

"The Witch raised me and cared for me as if I were her own." Ghost shrugged the shoulder not buried under Njall's large hand. "I don't know where she found me, or why I was there, but she's done me no harm, ever. All I know is I would have died if she hadn't rescued me."

Njall nodded. "Ghost was most fierce in his defense of the Witch when we spoke."

"And of course, you believed him." Bruadar's words were accompanied by a sneer. Ghost felt his temper rising.

"He gave me no reason to disbelieve him. He spoke as I would have spoken, if someone had insulted Falkor to my face." Njall's fingers tightened a little on Ghost's shoulder. This time, Ghost knew he was being cautioned.

The soft voice confirmed Ghost's suspicions. *There's something wrong about Bruadar. If you look hard, you can see it. You're like me. You can see inside.*

Ghost resisted the urge to turn and look at Egill. The Witch was not a seer, and certainly Njall was not talking inside his head in such a small voice. Nothing about Njall was small. Ghost suddenly understood why the Witch had Egill with her, and why Bruadar had raised Ghost's hackles from the moment Ghost had laid eyes on him. Egill, like Ghost, was a seer. So was Bruadar, but the shaman was masking the Sight. Egill felt it as wrongness, but Ghost's gift was more developed, and he *saw* it clearly. He wondered if the Witch knew what Bruadar was.

"Send the shaman away and I will speak," the Witch said. "I've told you, Falkor. I won't speak while he's here. If he's foolish enough to think I can do you any harm, then you should consider finding a wiser shaman."

Bruadar growled deep in his throat. "You should not be alone with this outlander woman, Falkor. It's not proper."

"I will be here," Njall said. "Unless you wish to cast doubt on my loyalty, shaman?"

Ghost held his breath, the tension in the room thick. Whatever game the Witch was playing, Njall was playing along. Ghost could not be sure if Njall knew the stakes or simply despised the shaman.

"Leave us, Bruadar." Falkor's voice was low, but it held enough authority and scorn to make Bruadar hold his tongue. "My son will see to my safety if it turns out I have need to fear a woman and two boys."

The heavy hand on Ghost's shoulder closed a little more, and Ghost refrained from turning around to glare at Njall. He did not need Njall's cautioning. Ghost was familiar enough with this game. He had seen the Witch bait the godsmen a double hand of times or more.

The moment the door closed behind Bruadar, the Witch turned her gaze to Falkor. "Now you shall have your answers, if you ask the right questions."

"You are fearless to bargain with me in my own hall." Falkor sat back. "I was told you slapped my son when he mistook you for a thrall. Is this so?"

"I am a hag. I no longer have the patience I once had for impetuous youth and even more impulsive appetites. But I'm inclined to be forgiving without your shaman glowering at me." The Witch gave Falkor a faint smile. "I found Ghost nearly nineteen autumns past. He couldn't have been more than a few months old, but his blanket was warm and well-made, and I could see he'd been loved and cared for. What reason, I wondered, could there be for a Norther dam to abandon a loved child? I looked to see if I could find the dam, thinking she might've been wounded, but I found no one else in the ruins. If there was a ranger about, he'd been prudent enough to avoid me."

Ghost listened, keeping silent. The Witch had never told him the exact circumstances under which he had been found, yet he could tell by her manner she was speaking the absolute truth.

Falkor's head lifted, the man still vital despite his age. "Only a shaman can call for a child to be cast out. If a child is marked by the gods as cursed, the child is left in the old places."

"And so we have a piece of the puzzle," the Witch said. "I was led to those particular ruins for a reason. I was meant to find this child and take him back with me to the village where I dwelled. The Seeker's hand was on me as I traveled." She gave Ghost a small smile before she turned back to Falkor. "I found a wet nurse for him, and he grew. But he cried each night as though the Sea brought him the darkest of dreams. I asked among my sisters, and one knew what to do for my little Ghost. She told me to mark him with peridot because the stones could soothe his dreams and awaken his inner eye. He was a seer, this small and fierce babe, and it seems the shamans fear the gift, or at least one shaman does. We witches do not."

Falkor turned to Ghost, his faded blue eyes sharp. "Is this true?"

"I can't tell you how I was found, but I'm a seer. The Seeker sends me visions, and I have to unravel what they mean. I can also diagnose the sick, but I control *seeing* disease and injuries, unlike the visions." Ghost stopped and shook his head. "I can push for a vision, but it won't always be granted, and it takes a lot out of me. It hurts to *see* that way, but I serve the Seeker."

Njall's fingers loosened on Ghost's shoulder but the Norther did not release him. Ghost glared at Njall and turned back to Falkor.

"I don't have any powers to harm you. The shamans lied if they told you otherwise. Well, unless *seeing* the truth is dangerous." Ghost shrugged free of Njall's grip, irritated by his proximity.

"The truth can be a danger," Falkor said. His voice was more tired than angry. "The truth is often inconvenient when you are trying to protect your people."

Ghost was not even close to mollified. "How do you protect your people? By leaving an inconvenient babe in the ruins? Not that the Heartlands is idyllic. We have orphans, and they're not always cared for as well as they could be. But we don't leave them for the sind to eat."

"Or to be found by a ranger who trades in slaves." The Witch's voice was harsh with anger. Ghost blinked at the open show of emotion from her. "Ghost was lucky the Seeker guided me to him. She wasn't so kind to Egill."

Egill stood between the Witch and Ghost. He looked startled at the mention of his name and shrank back, only to bump into Njall. He opened his mouth in a mute plea and scurried around Ghost to put Ghost between himself and Njall.

"Be still, child. No one here will hurt you. I've given you my word." The Witch's voice grew gentle, and Ghost put an arm around Egill.

"What happened to him?" Falkor seemed resigned to hearing an answer he would not like. His faded blue eyes held grief, although his face remained impassive.

The Witch replied in a strong voice. "As far as we've been able to tell, Egill was nearly eight years old when the slave traders found him. He'd been left to fend for himself for who knows how long. Egill isn't sure. The slave traders took him to the West Reaches and traded him into the household of a certain witch who doesn't find it agreeable for her slaves to talk. Egill was trapped in that hellish household for two years, after his voice was stolen from him. Two years until he was rescued by a brave witch." The Witch's dark eyes shone with tears, and Ghost stared at her in consternation. Ghost had never seen her cry before this moment. "He's under my protection now. I promise you, Falkor, I won't let him be harmed any more than he has been already." She met Egill's eyes and her expression softened. "I gave him my oath."

"Why do the shamans fear us?" Ghost spoke without thinking, angered by the fear radiating from Egill. The boy was tense, and Ghost held him tighter. "What have we ever done to hurt them? I was a fucking babe. What was I going to do, piss on them? Egill was just a small child. We were defenseless."

Njall's laughter rolled out like spring thunder, and he offered a sheepish shrug when Ghost rounded on him. "I am sorry, little Ghost. You are as fierce as any warrior when roused, truly, and I cannot picture you as defenseless, even as a babe." Njall grew serious. "But the question you ask is valid, and I would also like to hear the reasons." He turned to his father.

"I cannot answer the why of it. Only the shamans can tell you why the children who have such a curse are left in the deserted places. Most of them are already well past infancy when the curse is discovered. The babes are the lucky ones, I think. But they do not last long, those babes." Falkor shuddered. "Bruadar told me one of my own sons bore the curse. I took him from his mother's breast and laid him in the deserted place with my own hands. I listened to his cries grow weaker through the night, until I heard nothing but silence in the dark. His mother cursed me, and stabbed me when I took him from her. But how could I defy the gods and bring their wrath down on all my clan? She fled into the snows with my blood on her knife, and I never saw her again, nor have I known joy since that night."

"Bruadar's held that night against you, hasn't he?" Ghost felt the heat in his spiral. "He said you were weak when you sat there all night, but he promised not to tell anyone if you made him your chosen shaman. He thinks he has power over you, but there's nothing weak about loving a child. Love is the kind of strength he'll never know, Falkor."

Egill moved closer to Ghost, his slight frame fitting under Ghost's arm easily. *Ask Falkor how Bruadar can tell.* The soft voice was insistent, and Ghost took a breath.

"How does Bruadar know a child is cursed?" Ghost felt Njall's hand fall on his shoulder again, a light touch this time, and he turned his head to glare at the tall warrior. "If you say one word to me about outlanders not asking questions, I'll find a way to shrivel your cock that can't be undone. Trust me on this."

The Witch snorted, but she looked at Falkor with her fierce, dark eyes, and Ghost let out his breath in relief.

"It's a good question, Falkor. Do you simply let Bruadar have his way, or do you demand proof?" The Witch lifted her chin and regarded Falkor with icy calm.

"How does one prove such a thing?" Falkor looked away. "Bruadar said the gods told him."

"I can say my gods sent me here," Ghost said. "Saying the words doesn't make them true, though. How do I prove something exists when all I have is dreams and jumbled riddles only I *see* and hear? The proof comes when what I say will happen actually does happen. How many of the cursed children were the children of your supporters?"

Njall growled, but Falkor held up his hand. "The outlander has a valid point. Some of my strongest warriors' children were cast out. I did not see a pattern until now, until the outlander spoke his truth." He turned to the Witch. "But this child who accompanies you. Him, I do not know. He is not of my clan."

Egill drew closer to Ghost, his pale eyes wide as he stared up at Falkor. The Witch broke the growing silence.

"Egill had crucial information I needed." The Witch didn't bother to explain further, and Falkor didn't ask. "My sister Tal found Egill, and she risked her life to bring him out of that hell he was in. She called in favors and lied when she had to, but she smuggled Egill past the watchers and sent him to me for protection. The rest is witchsister business and not for you to hear."

Falkor raised his hand to rub his eyes. "If the child cannot speak, how will you learn your information?"

"I have my ways." The Witch looked at Falkor, her expression fearless. "Egill will leave when I do. I'm not bringing trouble to your clan. I want to meet with a healer who can teach me about certain Norther herbs. I'll offer a fair trade for such herbs, and we'll all leave without any more fuss. Bruadar wanted to refuse me. I think Falkor is wise enough to do what's best and not follow where Bruadar wants to lead."

Ghost managed not to snort at the heavy-handed flattery, but Falkor seemed to think the Witch's words were fine. Perhaps he merely succumbed to the relief of hearing the Witch offer to leave.

"Njall, bring this woman to meet a healer. Instruct the healer to deal in fairness with the outlander." Falkor inclined his head toward Ghost. "You will stay. I wish to speak with you further."

It did not sound at all like a question, and Ghost bristled. "Why do we have to speak alone?"

The Witch stiffened, and Egill trembled against Ghost. He could not blame Egill for being afraid. Egill's life had been miserable since he was cast out, and now that he had found a measure of security with the Witch, Ghost was stirring up more trouble. Ghost glared at Falkor as he waited for a response.

"You are a guest in these halls. You have eaten meat at my table, and your safety is my obligation." Falkor sighed and gestured to Njall.

Njall reached out to take Egill by the shoulder, but Egill did not flinch away as he had earlier, when the Witch had touched him. He put his arms around Ghost's waist and held tight, his expression defiant.

"Child." The Witch spoke in a gentle voice. "We'll wait for Ghost outside. As I understand it, guest law prohibits Falkor from harming Ghost, or allowing him to be harmed." The Witch gazed at Falkor and her eyes were unreadable. "We will simply have to hold Falkor to that, won't we?"

Egill allowed Ghost to transfer him into the Witch's arms, but his eyes were on Ghost. *If you need help, I'll hear you.* Ghost smiled at Egill with as much reassurance as he could muster.

Falkor watched Njall escort the Witch and Egill from the room. When the door closed behind them, he turned his gaze on Ghost.

"The truth is often obscured, young witch. Not all of the exiled children were sons of my chosen warriors. Some were children whose fathers named themselves my enemies," Falkor said, his voice low. "Bruadar is not one of the Norther people. A hunting party found him among the wagons and frozen bodies of a trading caravan. The hunters claimed the goods and brought the child home because they believed the gods had spared him for a reason. Many attempts were made to foster him, yet each family returned him. None could say why they would not have him. He has always made others uneasy."

Ghost suppressed a shudder as he listened.

Falkor continued speaking as though he had noticed nothing. "Finally, the shamans took Bruadar in, and he was raised to be one of them. He had faced death and returned, and they believed the hand of the gods was on him. Bruadar seemed happy enough among the shamans, and so it has been. His advice was sound, and the gods favored him, as did I."

"And now?" Ghost asked, watching as Falkor stood and stepped down from the platform. "Will you still favor him?"

"I do not know." Falkor looked older than when Ghost had walked into the room. "In my dreams, my son speaks to me, the one I left in the deserted place. He tells me we will meet again, and he is with his mother. He tells me not to fear death. But I do fear it, Ghost of the witches. I fear the gods will find me lacking because I left him to die."

"I can't give you the reassurances you want, and I won't ask to *see*." Ghost folded his arms. "Not right now. I have a village full of sick people, and my obligation is to my patients. I'll come back in the summer, if you'd like."

"In the summer?" Falkor gave Ghost a tired smile. "Is your blood so thin, like an outlander's?"

"Yes," Ghost retorted. He did not return the smile. "But for now, I want to rejoin the Witch and Egill. We have a lot to discuss about the epidemic devastating my village and how we're going to stop the disease and cure the afflicted."

"Go to the library. I will ask her to meet you." Falkor's smile had faded like his eyes.

Chapter Fifteen

GERRY ASSISTED NATALI as best he could. It was the only way he could think of to apologize to Ghost. In the four days since Ghost had left, Gerry had ample time to regret his rash words. He would do what he could in his beloved witch's absence and hope that Ghost would forgive him.

He returned home late in the evening. Between Natali and Ghost, Gerry was well-trained. As tired as he was, he headed for the washhouse to scrub and change into clean clothing since he had not washed at the infirmary. He had been exhausted all day, and toward evening, his head had begun to ache, enough to be annoying.

Dealing with the sick had not gotten much easier for Gerry. He could handle the older villagers well enough, but it was always the babes who got to him. The young woman who was pregnant had not survived, and despite all Natali's best efforts, the babe had gone with the dam. Gerry had seen Natali cry for the first time, fatigue and grief warring for dominance in the witch's sobs. Merrah had taken Natali into the workroom, soothing her with gentle words. Seeing the toll of the stress on Natali reminded him too much of how he had gotten it so wrong with Ghost.

Gerry's headache grew steadily worse, and his stomach roiled. Maybe he had contracted the plague? He supposed it was inevitable, given how much time he spent at the infirmary and no matter how well he had scrubbed. He was young and strong, and if the sickness held true, he would have a bad night, maybe a day in bed, and he would be fine.

Gerry dried off and dressed. He shivered uncontrollably, although his skin felt hot to the touch. The fever was making itself known, and Gerry hurried back to the house after collecting the bucket he used for offal, in case he needed to purge. A good night's sleep was what he needed, although sleep was elusive without Ghost beside him. Gerry had become accustomed to Ghost, and Ghost's absence left his soul restless. He set the kettle on the hearth fire to heat while he added wood and went to see if there were any of the packets Ghost had made to treat the infection. He was a witch's mate. He should be able to make the infusion by now.

GHOST LEFT FALKOR'S audience room, lost in thought. He struggled to comprehend the motivation behind Bruadar's actions concerning the children who had been sent to their deaths. Bruadar was a seer, just as much as Ghost and Egill were, but the knowledge offered no justification for Bruadar to seek out and condemn children who were also seers. Encouraging them to become shamans, to build a strong fellowship as the witches had done, made more sense. Certainly, Falkor seemed to rely on Bruadar's advice despite Bruadar being an outlander, as Falkor put it. Ghost wondered if Bruadar's ability to *see* made him valuable to Falkor, or if Bruadar had tried to repress his gift. The unanswered question was whether all the shamans were seers or if this was only Bruadar's secret.

"It is folly to walk with one's head in the clouds."

Ghost regarded Bruadar dispassionately, not surprised to encounter the shaman again. "It depends, doesn't it? Much can be seen up there, but it's a lousy place to hide. Clouds can be blown apart by a good wind."

Bruadar snorted, his face set in a frown. "Do witches like to speak in riddles?"

"No more than shamans do," Ghost replied. Ghost did not fear Bruadar as much now that he knew what Bruadar was. "My gift as a seer allows me to heal. I use it to *see* below the surface to determine the cause of the symptoms my eyes show me. What do you use your gift for, beyond hunting down other seers?"

Bruadar looked surprised by Ghost's blunt words. "What gives you grounds to accuse me?" He drew himself up, his dark clothing rustling around him.

Ghost smiled. "It's not an accusation. It's an observation, and one that didn't take my gift to *see*. You're scared of what you are. The question I still have is why? Why do you tell Falkor the gods want children with the Sight left to die?"

"Outlanders do not—"

"Ask questions. I know and I don't care. I told Njall to stop telling me not to ask questions too." Ghost shook his head. "I'm Norther born, but raised as an outlander, while you're outlander born and raised among the Northers. Neither one of us has room to poke at the other. So I'll just ask what I like, and you can answer as you choose."

"I might choose not to answer at all, whelp," Bruadar growled.

"True enough, and if this was solely about me, I wouldn't really push." Ghost moved to corner Bruadar, a subtle crowding he had seen Gerry use in the market when trade was very busy. "But Egill? You owe me answers for his sake, and there's more than one way to ask. My mate wouldn't approve, but he's not here to remind me to be civilized. The fear in Egill's eyes just might influence me to use methods best left to a Wester or a renegade slaver. He's only a little boy. No child should have that much terror to remember."

Ghost paused, seeing Bruadar's expression waver a fraction. "You were afraid too, when you realized what you could do. Not to mention how you made people feel afraid. I'm pretty sure it's why the Witch raised me outside the village. I needed to learn how to control the gift and not *see* into everyone I met."

"Why do you call it a gift? The Sight is a curse, a mark of the gods' disfavor." Bruadar's voice was low, and his dark eyes raked Ghost. "The gods did me no kindness. I watched the faces of the people harden, and they turned away from me in loathing."

"Because they didn't understand," Ghost insisted. "No one understood your needs. I was lucky the Witch comprehended enough to know what I needed. The Sight isn't an easy gift, but it isn't a curse. When you were sent to the shamans, your life got better, didn't it? They weren't afraid of you. They taught you to control the Sight. And look how you've repaid them, by trying to kill every child with the Sight you discovered. Have the gods rewarded you, or are you suffering every night when you *see* those small ones in your dreams?"

Bruadar looked at Ghost for a very long moment, as if he was deciding something. Finally, he nodded abruptly. He gestured for Ghost to follow him. They walked through the halls in silence until they came to a dark wooden door. Bruadar paused with his hand on the latch.

"You are a guest in these halls and have eaten the food of the clan," Bruadar said. The words carried a grave formality. "Before the gods, no harm will come to you at my hands."

Bruadar opened the door and walked into the room, and Ghost followed without hesitation. He looked around in open curiosity. A low fire burned in a small hearth in the otherwise dark room, sending shadows dancing in the corners. The furnishings were austere, and Ghost stared at the strings of charms and talismans hung from the walls, including what he guessed were the bjarrn teeth Njall had mentioned. Ghost sat on a bench and waited to hear what Bruadar wanted to tell him. While he wanted to speak to the Witch, he also needed to know what had motivated Bruadar, and perhaps other shamans as well. Bruadar held the missing pieces of his past as well as Egill's.

"You call yourself a witch, but you speak as if you are a servant of the gods." Bruadar stirred the fire and added a thick knot of wood. "Do you serve your gods, or is it simply so many words?"

Ghost watched the shadows draw back from the growing fire. "The Seeker sends me visions so I can do what she needs me to do. I've seen the gods' hands in my life. I'd be an idiot not to revere them and serve them faithfully, even if I sometimes doubt the godsmen always speak the truth."

"And the witches? Do they speak the truth?" Bruadar sounded haunted.

"The Witch does, and a few I trust as much." Ghost ignored the faint warmth growing behind his spiral. "Some witches haven't earned trust. Like anyone else, they have factions and circles. Some think no male should be a witch, and they hate me solely for being male. So, I suppose it would depend on who was doing the talking."

Bruadar examined the flames. "Do witches have the power to curse a man?"

Ghost's head whipped around at Bruadar's question. "I could tell you yes, but that wouldn't be entirely accurate. Yes, a witch can curse someone, and yes, the curse might even affect them, but only if they believed in the curse's power. If they didn't, then the curse would just be words."

"You offered to curse Njall's manhood," Bruadar countered. His eyes looked haunted.

Ghost snorted. "I offered to shrivel it. I know herbs that can do a good job, or maybe he believed me too. If not, then it was just more words."

Bruadar seemed to ponder Ghost's words, and Ghost wondered if the Witch had threatened him. It would not be unlike her at all. She could be fierce when she wanted, but he doubted she had gone quite so far with Bruadar. The Witch wanted information, and Bruadar had what she desired. She was not likely to lose sight of her goal.

"Your Witch is not the first of her sisterhood I have met." Bruadar looked into the fire as he spoke, and he appeared pensive. "Another one came to the clanhold. Last summer. She had a triple moon in blue ink on her forehead. She wanted use of the books collected here by the leaders of the clan. Falkor agreed she could come to consult them."

"What was she looking for? Did she say?" Ghost focused on Bruadar's words. His witchmark grew warmer, and he wondered if the Seeker was warning him to take heed. He did not know the marking Bruadar described, but he would ask the Witch later, in private.

"I do not think she wanted anyone to know, but I saw some of the books she read. She sought knowledge of certain machines used when the cities were still alive. I do not know if such machines still exist, or if they died with the cities." Bruadar's expression was somber. "She saw me looking at the books she had read, and she told me if I spoke of this to another, I would face her curse. She said I would beg for death before she was done with me. I have seen death once, and I do not fear it. I fear being held on the edge of it, in the grip of pain and madness."

"Unless she could reach out across distances and touch you, I don't think you have a lot to worry about." Ghost knew he sounded far from reassuring. "I believe she was trying to frighten you into keeping quiet. If a witch was really serious about silencing you, you'd be dead already."

Bruadar seemed taken aback by Ghost's words. "The witches kill so lightly?"

"No." Ghost watched Bruadar relax a little. "But when the witches do take a life, they make it serve as a warning. Most often the rangers need the reminder from time to time."

"These rangers, who are they?" Bruadar asked.

"Rangers search the ruins looking for relics and lost lore. They trade for what they need. Healing, sometimes, or goods they can't hunt or scavenge. They have a guild that makes law for the rangers, but some rangers can't follow even their scant law and they're exiled. The exiles steal children to trade as slaves, or rape and kill." Ghost was reminded of Bernd, and he tried not to shudder.

"Thralls of the slavers. The warriors kill them on sight here. They only come in the summer." Bruadar sounded satisfied, and Ghost frowned.

"We're happy enough to let them scavenge the ruins and trade for what they find." Ghost shrugged, dismissing the topic of rangers. "Will you show me the books the other witch read?"

"I gave the books to Eir, one of our healers, and told her to give them to your Witch. As she reminded me, the ways of witches are not for me to know."

Ghost had expected protest. The easy agreement made Ghost wary, and he glanced at his hands to hide his expression. "Thank you."

"Despite the impression you may have, the business of a shaman is not to take life." Bruadar's voice was dry, and Ghost was reminded of the Witch on the verge of a lecture. "Do you know how to determine if you have been called to be a shaman?"

"You're the first one I've met, so I have no idea." Ghost looked up again, interested in spite of himself.

"A shaman has met death at some point and may even have crossed over, only to return. The shamans decided I had met death when I was the sole survivor of a trading caravan caught in an early snow." Bruadar shrugged one shoulder. "I was a babe then, but in dreams, I have recalled the meeting. The brush with death makes me a shaman. You have met death as well. I can *see* it."

Ghost growled and reached for his belt knife, meaning to prick his finger, but the knife was gone. He bit his lip hard instead and turned his head to spit blood-streaked saliva into the fire. "Avert your eyes and pass me by," he muttered, offering the ritual blood to the Seeker's dread mate. "The Witch found me abandoned in a ruin, so maybe. I don't know. I've never asked to *see* why I was thrown away, and I'm not ready to give up on living. I have a mate and a life waiting for me." Ghost reveled in a warm rush of love at the mere mention of his mate, and a growing elation at the prospect of being back in Gerry's embrace where he belonged.

"Your tests are not over, Ghost of the Heartlands, Ghost of the witchsisters." Bruadar's voice rang like the voices in Ghost's visions, and despite the warmth of the fire, Ghost's spine turned to ice. "Ask the one who taught you. The witches count in threes. Twice you met death, and twice you earned a name. One more test waits for you."

Ghost spat again, his heart thudding in his chest. He knew exactly what Bruadar meant. He was supposed to have died as a babe in the ruins, but the Witch found him and brought him to the Heartlands instead. Bernd would have killed him once the exiled ranger had worked up the courage, and Gerry rescued him that time. Bruadar's dark eyes had glazed over, and Ghost watched as Bruadar shook off the vision with a shudder.

"What else did you *see*?" Ghost asked, hearing the strain in his own voice. Bruadar's vision brought him back to reality. The third test had to be the epidemic. While Ghost was indulging his curiosity in this dark and timeless room, the afflicted in his village were dying. He needed to find the Witch and her solution. He stood up, the bench scraping on the floor from his haste. "Did you *see* my village? I don't have my mirror, so if you've *seen* my people, I want to know."

Bruadar's laugh was bitter. "You of all people should know better than to ask. Do we ever *see* what we desire most?"

GERRY WOKE TWICE in the night to vomit, and his head pounded. He was weak enough the second time to resort to his bucket. His teeth chattered as he fell back onto the bed. He could not even find the strength to rinse his mouth with cold water. He pulled up the quilt, shivering and miserable.

As he fell into a fitful sleep, Gerry dreamed Ghost's warm hand stroked his forehead. He could hear Ghost's quiet voice soothing him. He grew warmer, and the terrible shivering eased until he found himself soaked with sweat. He tossed the quilt aside as he tried to cool off.

His stomach seized again, and Gerry rolled off the bed to find the bucket. The floor was rough beneath his knees as he vomited, tasting blood mixed with bile. When the fit had passed, the shivering began again. Gerry could hardly manage to crawl back onto the bed. Exhaustion dragged him under before he could find the quilt. The sheets beneath him were clammy and cold.

"WHAT HAVE YOU found?"

The Witch was not alone. Egill shadowed her, of course, and the Norther healer, Eir, was with her too. Ghost marked his place with a scrap of fabric and closed the book with care.

"No doubt the same as you found," Ghost said. He shrugged one shoulder. "The lore is curious on its own, but there's more I don't know yet."

"We never know everything." The Witch looked amused. "Eir has been good enough to give me some herbs that should prove useful." She gestured at the quiet woman at her side. "Have you made notes as you've been reading?"

Ghost gestured at his formulary with ink-stained fingers. His careful writing covered almost two pages. "I always make notes, precisely as you taught me. I haven't forgotten."

An excessive friendliness in the Witch's tone made Ghost cautious. He snuck a glance at Egill from under his lashes, and Egill returned the look with wide eyes.

"Wonderful," the Witch said. "I'll give you my notes on the local herbs to copy later. Come by my room and you can borrow my formulary."

The Witch's offer sounded utterly natural. Of course, no witch ever handed over her formulary other than to an apprentice and even then it was often carefully edited first, but Ghost did not think Eir would know the truth. He looked up with what he hoped was a bright smile. "Thank you, I'd appreciate seeing your notes as well."

It was true. Ghost did want a chance to talk to the Witch in private. Until he did, he could not tell friend from foe, and too much was at stake to risk it. But after leaving Bruadar, he had gotten turned around, and by the time he had found the library, he assumed he had missed her.

The Witch continued in the same artificial tone. "With any luck, we can all be on our way soon. I know you want to get home so you can see your mate again."

She doesn't want to talk about the sickness. Egill's soft voice confirmed what Ghost suspected. The Witch's caution made him nervous.

"Lady smile on us, and Father see us safely home," Ghost said. He hoped his response seemed bland enough, although his words were true. Ghost wanted to be on his way home, back to Gerry and to his village. He would be happier if he had answers to all his questions, but at this point, he was willing to wait until they were on the carriage to hear what the Witch had learned. Some force, or perhaps some person, had stopped her when she had first contacted Ghost. He was not sure he wanted to face anything that stumped her.

The Witch patted Ghost's shoulder. "And the Seeker guide our steps along the way," she replied. "Why don't you and Egill go to my room? You can start copying the formulary while you wait. Egill knows the way. Eir, about those herb samples? I'd love to get cuttings as well. Is this possible?"

Ghost stood and gathered up the books he had been reading. Egill waited by the door until Ghost was ready, and they set off through the corridors. The maze of hallways all looked alike to Ghost, but Egill moved with assurance, and Ghost was reminded Egill had lived in such a place not so long ago.

The Witch occupied a generous chamber filled with plenty of light from the windows along one wall. A scrubbed wooden table held books and sheets of paper covered in her cramped writing, the letters tiny enough to make Ghost squint. Egill crossed to the fire and prodded it, adding wood until the flames were leaping again. He gestured at the kettle, but Ghost shook his head.

Ghost opened the chest at the foot of the bed, rummaging among the Witch's unfamiliar shifts in their rainbow of colors until he found the worn leather pouch she always carried. "There we are."

Egill cleared a place for Ghost at the table, and Ghost looked at the boy. "You don't need to fuss over me. I don't expect it, you know." He opened the pouch and pulled out the Witch's formulary, turning to the back to see her recent notes. He saw quite a few on Norther herbs and even more speculating on what was going on in the village. Ghost's pen scratched as he copied the notes to his own formulary.

When his hand began to cramp, Ghost put his pen down and sat back. Egill was watching him, the boy's expression a mixture of curiosity and amazement. Ghost stood and stretched.

"Have you read her notes?" Ghost asked.

Egill nodded, and his small, pale fingers touched the rich leather of the books Ghost had brought with him.

"You read those too?" Ghost was surprised, but if Egill had lived among the Northers until he was seven or eight, he would have been taught to read. The Northers did not scorn books or the knowledge contained in the yellowed pages. Only the godsmen abhorred knowledge.

"Egill is adept at reading." Ghost spun around, startled to see the Witch enter and close the door behind her. "We were fortunate no one realized he was able to read where he wound up. Please don't tell me you didn't guess."

"So, they were right? The epidemic's not a natural illness?" Ghost felt his stomach twist. "Kerree said the disease seemed artificial, and she mentioned relics. Zereda hushed her, but the books I read described devices like centrifuges that can combine phages and bacteria to cause illness."

"Phages and viruses, yes." The words rolled off the Witch's tongue with ease. "The mistake Sri made was in letting Egill see her notes. She assumed he was an ignorant child, and although she made sure he could never speak about anything he heard, she never stopped to think he might know how to read and write. She and Tarah of the Heartlands contrived this epidemic, to discredit you and indirectly to discredit me, since I was your mentor."

Ghost stared at the Witch. "Tarah. Is her mark a triple moon in blue?"

"Did you see her?" The Witch's voice sharpened, and Egill flinched. Ghost reached out to pull him close.

"Bruadar told me she was here reading these books last summer." Ghost studied Egill, smoothing the boy's hair to calm him. "She was learning how to use the relics they found, but how could they do something like this? So many have died." Ghost was dumbfounded at Sri and Tarah's callousness. "I told Bruadar witches don't kill without reason. I was wrong."

"Tal was the first to figure it out, but she couldn't find proof, or the cure. Egill was smart enough to realize Tal was an ally, and he slipped her a note. Egill knew what Sri and Tarah had used to make the vector, and he knew about the cure they had devised. The plan was to wait until more people had died and the disease had progressed to killing those who thought they were immune. They were going to show up and cure the illness that the incompetent male pretender couldn't handle." The Witch chuckled. "Tal got Egill out, but the only place she could think of to hide him was here, in the Northlands, where he'd blend in. I intercepted his carriage and joined him. A fortunate choice, because some of the herbs we need are rare and there's one in particular that will grow nowhere else but here. Egill took what vials of the vaccine and antidote he could find, but we'll need more than what he was able to bring us."

Ghost touched the books. "The vision. 'What is known is lost. What is lost must be found.' These books have the knowledge we've lost." Ghost paused and looked at Egill. "And you found Egill."

The Witch agreed. "Finish the thought, Ghost." Her eyes shifted to Egill as he settled next to Ghost. "Seeker knows you're not my little one anymore."

Ghost took a deep breath. "The last part. 'What is found is the way home.' We have a cure, don't we? We can help the village and end this nightmare. Time to go home."

Chapter Sixteen

IN THE MORNING, Njall escorted Ghost, Egill, and the Witch through the snow-scarred landscape until they reached the end of a valley. A low wall marked the end of the clan's lands. Most of the wall was hidden, and only the stone posts rose far enough out of the frost to flaunt the witchmarks carved into their sides.

"This is as far as I will go." Njall's voice was the usual deep thunder, with a hint of laughter running through his words. He threw back the hood of his white fur cloak. "You are sure you know your way from here? I would not want to have to thaw out a Ghost again. He is most irritable in the morning."

Ghost pushed back the hood of his cloak, which had been returned to him along with his water skin and his pouches. He was happiest to have his cloak, his reminder of how much Gerry loved him. He had been offered a white fur cloak like Egill and the Witch wore, made of the soft fur of the viksin. He refused that gift, but he did accept boots lined with warm fur, and he found himself glad of those.

"Don't even dream about it," Ghost said, and his voice was sharper than he had intended. "I mean, I appreciate the intent and all, but I have a mate. I'm not cranky in the mornings with him either."

The Witch snorted. "I know the way, Njall, son of Falkor. You have been a generous host."

Ghost shifted the pouch on his shoulder. The Witch was right. Njall and Falkor had insisted they accept gifts, and Ghost's pouch held several more books about herbal lore and the medical technology of the ancients. Egill carried the cloak Ghost had refused, since Njall decided Ghost could give the cloak to Gerry. The Witch had her cuttings and herbs along with the vials from Egill and whatever else filled her own traveling pouch.

Bruadar had given Ghost a small amulet made from a bjarrn's tooth. Ghost suspected the tooth was the gift of one shaman to another, and he accepted the amulet with the gravity such a gift deserved. Ghost had given Bruadar his notes and observations on being a seer, Ghost sure he could recreate those from memory. The notes included the ritual to invoke a vision and instruction on making the smoke bundle to awaken the inner eye. Bruadar had accepted Ghost's notes with equal respect. Unspoken between them was the knowledge that Bruadar would work to create a haven for Norther seers, his penance for the lives he had taken.

But now the time had come to go, and Ghost was eager to return to his village and to Gerry. Farewells had to be said first, though, and he watched the Witch offer Njall her hands, wrapped in mitts lined with more viksin fur. Njall's hands were bare and engulfed hers.

"You are always welcome in our clanhold, Witch," Njall said, and he hugged the Witch, lifting her off her feet for a moment. "I like a woman who is not afraid to slap me."

"You have a remarkable aptitude for provoking me into slapping you," the Witch said in a voice as dry as dust. "You should be glad I haven't taken you up on your offers."

Njall turned to Ghost, and Ghost placed his mitt-covered hands in those large palms.

"You too are always welcome in our clanhold, little Ghost." Ghost gasped as Njall's strong arms closed around him. "If your mate is not good to you, come and let me warm you." Njall purred the offer, his breath tickling Ghost's ear.

Ghost was sure his cheeks were hot enough to melt the snow feathering down from the tall trees and dusting them in white. "I don't think I'll have to worry about Gerry not being good to me, but thank you. I think."

Egill seemed to be trying to hide behind the Witch, but Njall turned to the boy. "While our clan is not yours, you would have a place in our clanhold if you wished to return to us, Egill of the Northlands. I cannot make amends for the wrongs perpetrated against you, but I can offer a better future as my foster son."

Egill shook his head and reached out to touch the Witch with a mitt-covered hand. Egill looked at Ghost, his expression pleading.

"We'll look after him," Ghost said. He watched relief light up Egill's eyes, and he was reminded of the child in his vision with blood pouring from his mouth. The posts of the boundary wall looked like the stones in the snow, and the Witch stood there in her cloak of white fur, her hair silvery against the stark, pale sky. For a moment, Ghost was dizzy, his head spinning as he realized the vision was not done with him, not yet. He had not *seen* Gerry in the vision, and his blood ran cold as he wondered if he had forfeited Gerry's love. Ghost could not endure a life without Gerry. Despite the warmth of his cloak, he shivered involuntarily.

THE CARRIAGE WAS warm, and the first thing the Witch did was to start the charging of the conveyance. Egill curled up on one padded bench, still wrapped in the viksin furs, while Ghost checked the compartment where he had found the healers' supplies. The container was empty.

"I've never seen one refilled, once the compartment was emptied. But we don't know how many carriages have survived. Every now and again, one appears that hasn't been ridden by one of us. You were lucky, but I know you'll make good use of what you found." The Witch offered Egill a cup of something hot that smelled delicious, and Egill took the cup with alacrity. She handed another cup to Ghost, who sniffed it.

"Broth," the Witch said. "To take the chill off. By the time we're ready for a meal, this carriage will be able to offer proper food. And before you ask, I don't understand how the carriage does it. All I know is if you recharge the carriage, you can get food. But while we wait, I want to contact Zereda. She can get the word out for us, although you may want to contact Natali yourself."

Ghost concurred. "I do want to talk to Natali. I'm going to give her one of the Seeker's kisses I found and some cylinders. I can show her how to refill the cylinders once the healers' supplies are used up. I want to thank Natali for all her hard work, along with giving her my promise to return the service if she needs me."

The Witch smiled. "Very good, Ghost. You've nothing to worry about, you know. You're doing extremely well. Most witches would not have dared to leave to find me, but this epidemic would not have been cured otherwise, and Sri would have won. Egill is part of the answer, but Falkor was not about to let me take him and go. He thought I was a slaver, or looking to steal the cursed children for some terrible rite, I think. The gods only know what nonsense Bruadar was filling his head with, really. But Egill is the key, in more ways than one." The Witch arched a brow. "Did you think I was cloaking myself to be difficult? Sri was looking for Egill, and no one had taught him how to hide yet. I cloaked us both. You never sensed Egill when I contacted you, but Sri was looking for me as well, it seems. That's why I cut you off so abruptly."

"What will happen to Sri?" Ghost could not shake his growing unease.

The Witch's expression hardened. "We have sufficient proof to make an example of her, one that will ensure no other witch makes a similar mistake. She broke every vow she took, and it can't go unpunished."

Ghost had watched many of his people perish at Sri's hands, and her actions were unforgivable. A witch vowed to help and to heal, and what Sri and her cabal had done was the opposite. Still, the Witch's tone promised Sri would end up begging for death, and Ghost was not hard-hearted. Beccah had done her best to help. He did not wish Sri's fate on Beccah.

"It's witch's business," Ghost said aloud, knowing he had no say in what the elder witches would decide. "What will we say to my village?"

"Once again, very good. You're learning, little one. We tell the village you reached out to the witchsisters and found a cure. Then you cure your people, Ghost, and they'll be proud of how their witch saved them." The Witch shrugged. "It's the truth, if no more than a part. They don't need to know about Sri and the devices she found and used in the West Reaches. The Wester land already has a bad reputation, thanks to the slavers."

"Beccah offered her help. I don't think she ever knew what was planned. I think we leave Beccah out of this. But the other one, Tarah, was in on the scheme from the start. She should share Sri's fate." Ghost looked over at Egill, who had finished his broth and was dozing on the bench, warm in his furs. "And him? What happens to him?"

"He has a choice to make. He's welcome to travel with me, although I can't promise I'll stay in one place too long. I'll teach him what I know, and Zereda can help with the rest." The Witch pinned Ghost with her dark eyes, and Ghost grew still. "Or you can find him a place in your village, and make sure he's cared for."

Ghost shook his head. "The only place he can go in the village is with Gerry and me. He's a seer, first of all, and he's got no voice. I'm going to guess we don't know how to fix this?"

"Sri was very thorough, I'm afraid. He might never speak again, but he's smart and learns fast. We'd never have had the antidote or the vaccine without him. I want to be sure he'll be taken care of properly." The Witch glanced at Egill, and Ghost recognized the look she used to give to him, when Ghost had been as young. A lifetime had passed since Ghost had felt childlike and innocent. Gerry had been right. Taking life changed something deep inside. Ghost wondered if Egill represented a chance to make amends for using the Seeker's rest. Ghost could nurture a life instead.

"I can't speak for Gerry, but I wouldn't mind having Egill as a part of our family." Ghost looked at Egill, white-haired and blue-eyed like he was. For the first time in his life, Ghost felt less different, less a freak. Gerry loved how Ghost was unique among the villagers, but having been in the Northlands now, Ghost wanted to see at least one other person who looked like him. And Egill was a seer as well, with the potential to be a witch. So rare, to have both gifts, and in another male. Ghost would never feel like an outcast with Egill there.

The Witch's smile conveyed her understanding and agreement. Ghost dug in his leather pouch for his scrying mirror. "How long will it be before we're home, do you think? I want to reach out to Natali. I can ask her to tell Gerry when to expect me." He settled himself on the other bench, opposite Egill, wondering if Egill would sense his scrying and maybe even join in.

"The carriage is taking a different route home. It's what I think they called a 'fast track' or perhaps it was 'express.' I can't recall. But either way, we should be at the terminal by high sun tomorrow, and at the village not much past dusk, I'd think." The Witch looked at the pad and frowned at the map before nodding briskly. "By dark for certain."

"Just one night on the carriage? Much better," Ghost said, and he felt a tingle of anticipation as he thought about being in his own bed with Gerry the next night. He unwrapped his mirror and focused his mind on Natali's purple starburst. Ghost could feel his own spiral warming as he let himself fall into the meditative state he needed to achieve, relaxing as he waited.

GERRY OPENED HIS eyes, the pain behind them as bad as if Moran were pounding on thick planks with a heavy mallet right beside his ear. Dawn was close, the indigo of the sky paling as the sun approached. He groaned as he tried not to move at all. He was freezing again despite the quilt covering him.

Gerry's mouth tasted of blood from the purging. He thought about getting up to get a cup of water, but his stomach twisted in response. He was not sure he would make it to the kitchen, not the way the room was spinning at the moment. He closed his eyes again and tried to will his stomach to subside.

When Gerry opened his eyes again, the sun was close to high. Sweat trickled over his skin, his tongue thick in his mouth. The headache was still there, taking second place to the way his stomach churned. He could feel the burn of bile at the back of his throat, and his tongue darted out in a vain attempt to moisten his cracked lips.

Gerry managed to sit up and push himself out of the bed. He swayed as he stood. He was lightheaded, and his vision was blurry, but he took a few stumbling steps forward. Momentum carried him past the door and into the main room. One hand against the wall to steady his progress, Gerry navigated his way to the front door.

Sunlight assaulted Gerry, and he felt the headache blast him with full force as he squinted against the brilliant light. The bucket from the well took forever to fill, and Gerry was trembling with exhaustion by the time he was done. He could smell the cool water, though, and his tongue seemed to swell even more. He carried the bucket into the house so he could dip up a cupful of the liquid. Gerry drank cup after cup, greedy for the moisture, until his stomach rebelled. He stumbled out into the yard again, heading for the washhouse, but he only got halfway before he fell to his knees. His stomach lurched, and watery blood poured from his mouth and nose onto the ground beneath him, splashing across the pavers.

Gerry stood on shaky legs and made his way back to the house. He knew all too well what the blood meant. He crawled into the bed and pulled the quilt over him. His skin hurt as the soft fabric slid over it, and tears of exhaustion dampened his lashes. If the gods were kind, he would not pass before Ghost returned so Gerry could have a chance to say goodbye to his precious Ghost.

"GHOST?" NATALI'S MENTAL voice sounded odd, and Ghost sat up a little straighter.

"Lady smile on you, sister," he said. "I'm on my way back, and I think I have a cure. How are the villagers? How many more have died?" As much as he wanted to ask about Gerry, he needed to be a witch first, and an anxious mate second.

"Seeker be thanked." Natali's relief was palpable. "You found the Witch, then?"

Ghost nodded before he remembered Natali couldn't see him. "Yes, I did, and we should be back before dark tomorrow night. How bad is the epidemic?"

"I won't lie. Not good. We lost the young dam and her babe, and I have a hand more who I don't think will last until then. I've eased the way for some, but I'm running low on the tincture." Natali's mental voice was weary. "I'd have asked Gerry to see if you had any in your home, but he hasn't come to the infirmary today. Perhaps he's hunting. If so, he'll be here soon, and I can ask then."

"I have some in my cabinet, in the drawer and not with the rest of the jars." Ghost sighed, disappointed to have missed Gerry. "When you see Gerry, tell him I'll be home tomorrow night, and I miss him. Tell him I love him."

"Of course, my brother." Natali's witchmark faded in the scrying mirror. "Father keep you, Ghost. We'll see you tomorrow night."

Ghost broke the contact and looked over at the Witch. She sat at the small desk with her own mirror, deep in conversation with Zereda. As the Witch related their findings aloud, Ghost found himself listening to fill in the last missing pieces.

"Who'd have thought Sri would have stumbled on a centrifuge? And to use such a powerful relic to do what?

Humiliate me and destroy Ghost because she couldn't stand the thought of a male witch?" The Witch paused, and Ghost found himself wishing he could hear Zereda's response. Zereda had been a staunch friend since he had taken his vows, and Ghost trusted her like a true sister. He had not been invited to the conversation, however. He would have to content himself with listening to the Witch.

"Hunter take her, she'd have killed Egill if she'd known he could read, never mind he's a seer. She paralyzed his vocal cords. If I can't reverse it, he'll never be able to utter a word. But he can communicate quite well in writing, which is sufficient for our needs right now. Sri and Tarah will be punished as soon as I can arrange for a hearing before the witchsisters." The Witch paused.

"They designed the illness very carefully, Zereda. As you suspected, they started with your little biting insect and the disease it carries. The initial phage was meant to mutate, to evolve into a more virulent form that would attack all the villagers, not solely the elderly and the very young. None of the usual remedies would work either. Their technique is as brilliant as it is abhorrent. They made sure to have a vaccine though, in addition to their cure. They weren't about to risk themselves when they showed up to 'rescue' the village."

The Witch continued. "Egill memorized the antidote and wrote it out for me. Even the cure was designed to be difficult. One of the component herbs grows only in the Northlands, and the antidote's not half as effective without it. Tarah added that touch when she was up there researching how to use the centrifuge to isolate the desired viruses. I have cuttings of the herb now, and I should be able to grow some. A potent febrifuge, far better than anything we have. Yes, vastly better than willow bark."

Ghost sighed and reached for the book of small stories Njall had given him. He caressed the red leather cover before opening the book. Ghost had not had a book of his own since the ones he had hidden in the ruins, in his little hiding place. He would have to keep these out of sight of the godsmen. Although as a witch, he did have certain privileges. Depending on whether or not the godsmen could read, he could pass the books off as healers' lore. The thought made him smile, and he dove into the first story.

WITH EGILL AND the Witch for company, the carriage trip passed quickly for Ghost. He decanted an ample supply of the antidote into cylinders for the Seeker's kiss. He wanted to be ready to begin as soon as they reached the village. Egill helped, deft at the task, until they both grew tired.

Egill stripped off his tunic in preparation for sleeping, and Ghost grieved for Egill as he took in the scars striping Egill's back, a catalog of Sri's abuse. Egill curled up on the bench bed with Ghost, and Ghost found himself hoping Gerry would agree to take Egill as a dependent. The boy was fast finding a place in Ghost's heart, and Ghost would find it hard to see Egill go elsewhere.

Ghost spent the following morning in a one-sided conversation, telling Egill about the village and some of the more notable characters who lived there. Ghost tried not to talk about Gerry too much, but the conversation managed to wind around to Ghost's mate so often, Egill gave a silent laugh when Gerry's name cropped up yet again. The Witch could not hear Egill, but his amusement made her smile.

Egill still had trouble believing the Heartlands did not countenance slavery. Ghost watched his eyes light up each time Ghost reassured him, and Ghost's heart ached all over again for what Egill had endured in his short life. Ghost promised the gods Egill would be happy as long as Ghost had any say.

They reached the terminal outside the ruins by high sun, and they were all relieved when they emerged into the late autumn daylight. Ghost was determined to set off for the village at once, unwilling to wait any longer than he had to before he would see Gerry again. He had put together a bundle for Natali— the Seeker's kiss and a goodly assortment of cylinders his gift to her. Ghost included a book of herbal lore as well, and the Witch chuckled.

"Natali will be urging you to wander, if you're going to gift her so well when you return." The Witch's smile was warm though, and Ghost relaxed and returned the grin.

"She deserves every bit. I left her and Gerry with this mess and ran off, and even if we have a cure, they were the ones who had to deal with the sick and the dying. Not an easy task for anyone to cope with," Ghost said. "You should take a Seeker's kiss too. I don't remember you having one."

"I don't and I will," the Witch said, amused. "But hold on to the rest. They could prove useful in the future. Someday, you'll have an apprentice of your own, and you'll be able to give them what they need to begin as a witch."

Ghost could not help looking over at Egill, who was gazing around in undisguised delight. He lowered his voice. "Do you think there's a chance for his voice to return?"

"The ancients could do a great deal, and if we look hard enough, we may find a way. I'm going to see what I can locate. I also intend to make sure I get my hands on the centrifuge and whatever else Sri and Tarah were using." The Witch looked at Egill as he scuffed through a pile of autumn leaves, for once acting like the child he was. "If there's a cure, I'll find it. In the meantime, he's bright and he manages to get his point across even without words. You could find worse as an apprentice."

Ghost shook his head. "I'm not sure he wants to be a witch, after Sri. I'd teach him what I know, though, gladly. Even if he doesn't want to be a witch, he's a seer. And I do want Gerry to take him in as a dependent. I'd love to have him as part of our family."

"Then don't close doors," the Witch advised. "Talk to your Gerry, and if he agrees, see how things go. Egill may surprise you by wanting to learn from you."

Ghost thought about what he could say to Gerry as they walked back to the village. He and the Witch took turns giving Egill a description of the highlights and pitfalls of the region. Egill looked askance at the ruins, and Ghost was not sure if he was relieved or disappointed when Egill did not seem eager to explore them. Then again, with all Egill had been through, Ghost was not really surprised at his caution.

AT DUSK, THEY found Natali waiting for them at the door of the infirmary. She waved as they approached, her eyes widening a little when she saw Egill. Relief made her smile a little too bright to be believable, and dark circles shaded her eyes. Ghost looked around for Gerry, his heart sinking when he did not spot his mate.

"We hurried, my sister. We've got the cure, and I'm ready to start treating our patients." Ghost patted the leather pouch slung over his shoulder. "We'll start with the worst cases. I have a Seeker's kiss for you and some cylinders of the antidote already prepared for it."

The Witch had loaded her Seeker's kiss with a cylinder of the antidote, and she nodded to Natali. "The faster we get this into them, the better. If they're too far gone, even this might not help, but we'll try. The Lady knows they all deserve a chance."

Inside the infirmary, Mai and Merrah looked up at Ghost with a welcoming smile. "We knew you'd be back," Mai said, and she hugged Ghost with shy enthusiasm. Her eyes widened at the sight of the Witch and Egill. "Oh, you have company!"

"We'll save the introductions for later." The Witch gestured to Merrah. "Good to see you again. The girl grew up well, I see."

Merrah led the Witch to the room with the dams and their babes. "She did indeed, and I thank the Lady every day. But you should start here, Witch. The dams are starting to catch the disease from the babes."

GHOST AND NATALI administered the cure to the patients in the larger room while the Witch treated the dams and babes with Merrah's help. Sri and Tarah had done their work well as far as the cure. Ghost could see the tension and pain leaving each patient as he pressed the Seeker's kiss to their skin. The crying of the babes subsided as the Witch worked in the next room. Ghost found one man, unconscious and cool to the touch. Ghost needed to *see* to make sure the man was still alive. He gave the man the cure, but he held out little hope for recovery.

"I wanted the Seeker's rest for him, but I was all out," Natali whispered, her voice full of sorrow. "There are more like him. I counted two hands' worth right before you arrived."

Conn arrived with Mother to give Natali some relief. Mai and Merrah left to return to their home, promising to be back in the morning. Much to Ghost's surprise, Sari arrived, looking far better than when Ghost had first met her. Gerry, however, had not been by the infirmary all day, and no one had seen him since he had left for home two days before. Now that the panic had subsided and the first round of cures had been administered, Ghost was finally free to seek him out.

The Witch did not argue with Ghost. "Egill and I will stay here for a time to watch over everyone. You go home to Gerry." The concern in her eyes sent a chill through him. "If you need me, send for me. I will come. But before you go, let me give you the vaccine." She pressed her Seeker's kiss to Ghost's arm. "Natali and I have had it as well. Now, go find your Gerry."

Ghost nodded as he rubbed his arm, not willing to trust himself to speak at the moment. It was unlike Gerry to have forgotten to send word he would not be helping. Ghost had never known his mate to be so thoughtless, and Gerry's absence sent his mind wandering to all sorts of terrible places. What if Gerry had gone hunting and was injured again? Without someone spotting, a sind hole could be hidden under the autumn leaf fall. This was how they had met, after all. The whelps would be grown enough now so the dam would not attack automatically, but sind were opportunistic hunters, and they would stalk a human if they thought he was weak enough. Or there might have been a renegade ranger, one who saw Gerry as an easy mark. Ghost's thoughts came full circle and back to his vision again, the vision without Gerry in it. All he could recall was the snow and the child bleeding.

The Witch interrupted Ghost's thoughts, patting his shoulder to get his attention. "Go, little one. You can walk and fret at the same time."

"I'm sure he's fine, and I'm just being an idiot," Ghost muttered. "I'll see you in the morning."

Chapter Seventeen

GHOST GAVE IN to his urge to run through the market and to the slate path leading to his house. The house was eerily quiet. No smoke came from the chimney, and the windows were dark. Ghost's stomach clenched with fear as he rushed through the door.

The smell of sickness overwhelmed him, and he struggled not to panic. "Gerry?" he called. His voice sounded too loud in the quiet house. The hearth was dark and cold. Ghost could wait to light a lamp; the moon's light was more than enough.

The bedroom door was open. Ghost stepped in, and the smell of sickness worsened. "Oh, Seeker," Ghost whispered, seeing a shape under the quilt. "Gerry? Love, it's me. I'm home."

Gerry offered no response, and Ghost tugged the quilt down. Gerry was ashen, his cheeks rough with stubble, and his lips were dry and cracked. Dark shadows surrounded his eyes, and the sheets and his pillow were stained with blood.

"Father, protect us," Ghost breathed as he fumbled in his pouch for his Seeker's kiss. "Oh, love, everything's going to be all right. I'm here. I found the Witch and she had the cure. The antidote is going to work. I promise. I'm not going to lose you."

Ghost's hand was steady as he pressed the Seeker's kiss against Gerry's stomach. He waited for the hiss to stop before he lifted the relic away. "I'm going to light the fire now. I'll be right back, love." He pulled the quilt up over Gerry and hurried back out to the main room.

The wood basket was nearly empty. Gerry was diligent about keeping wood in the house. He must have been sick for some time, Ghost realized. Ghost kindled the kitchen hearth first and lit the smaller hearth in the main room to warm the back of the house. He went out to the yard to fill the bucket from the well, and he wound up sluicing the path where Gerry had vomited blood with the first bucketful. By the time he came back in, the house was already warmer, and Ghost lit some candles so he could see to work.

"Broth. A weak broth, and of course there won't be fresh bread," Ghost muttered as he checked the larder. "He's probably been eating at the infirmary. That would make sense."

Running back to the infirmary was out of the question. Ghost was not leaving Gerry, but he thought of another way. He pictured Egill in his mind and whispered aloud, "Egill? Can you hear me?"

I hear you. Ghost was grateful for the soft-voiced response, and he took a shaky breath.

"My Gerry is sick. I gave him the antidote, but he needs some nourishment. My house is across the market and toward the trees. It has a green door, precisely the color of my witchmark." Ghost waited for Egill to answer.

I can do this. I can find you now because I know your voice. Egill sounded confident, to Ghost's great relief.

Ghost went back into the bedroom, taking a candle with him. The bedroom was warming fast, but Gerry was still shivering. Ghost pressed two fingers to the base of Gerry's neck. Gerry was hot to the touch, and his heartbeat was too fast for Ghost's liking.

"What's going on here?" Ghost asked, his voice not even a whisper. "Did the illness change? Is this part of the design?" He reached for his Seeker's kiss and adjusted it to give another half-dose of the antidote. If this was the second stage of the disease, Sri's notes called for the additional medicine as the remedy. Ghost sat on the edge of the bed and administered the Seeker's kiss again. Ghost's eyes were intent on Gerry, seeking any sign of recovery.

"I'm not going to lose you, no matter what. I'll challenge the Seeker's dread mate himself if need be, but you are not going to die while I draw breath, love." Ghost's voice was hardly even a whisper, and his throat ached with tears he refused to shed. He stroked Gerry's stubbled jaw, his fingers tracing the strong lines over and over. Gerry's eyelids fluttered, but he did not waken.

"The cure will work, love," Ghost said, tucking the quilt around Gerry as he spoke. "You'll recover quickly, and we can get something warm in you. Egill's bringing it. You'll like him, love. He's not yet ten summers, but he's smart, and he's such a brave kid. He survived the West Reaches, and he smuggled out the antidote. And the best part? He's a Norther, like me. Really, I'm not kidding. Wait until you see him." The chatter was mostly for Ghost's benefit, to calm his nerves as he waited to see if Sri had lied.

Ghost lifted his head when he heard the door open. "I'm in the bedroom, Egill. I'll be right out." He turned back to Gerry. "I'm going to go out to the main room for a moment. I'll be back before you know it, love. You rest, all right?" Gerry did not respond, not even the flicker of an eyelid, and Ghost's stomach twisted with fear.

Egill waited by the table. *I came as fast as I could.*

"Thank you," Ghost said. "Did the Witch give you the vaccine yet? You should have a dose to prevent you catching this illness."

Egill shook his head, his expression solemn. *I already had the vaccine to test it. Sri wanted to be sure she wouldn't get sick.* He looked over at the bedroom door. *Will he get better?*

Ghost blinked, taken aback by the way his vision grew blurry. His voice sounded odd to his own ears when he spoke. "He has to get better. I won't let this damned disease of Sri's take him away from me." He cleared his throat and brushed the back of his hand over his eyes before he continued. "Will you sit with him while I clean up?"

I can clean for you. Egill's mental voice was meek.

"I'll do it. He's sleeping right now, and we need to wait for his fever to break. The antidote simply needs to start working. Tidying up will keep me busy while I wait." Ghost walked into the bedroom, Egill on his heels. "Maybe when I'm done, you can help me get him into clean clothing and get fresh sheets on the bed. I can wash him too."

Egill bobbed his head and sat on the edge of the bed where Ghost indicated.

"He should sleep, but if anything changes, call for me. I'll come running. Trust me." Ghost managed a smile and patted Egill's shoulder. "Thank you."

Ghost picked up the bucket by the side of the bed, recognizing Gerry's offal bucket. Ghost surmised Gerry had known he was getting sick, but he had not tried to go back to the infirmary. The disease must have had a swifter onset than usual, which made Ghost even more certain the illness had changed as Sri and Tarah had intended. He wondered if Egill had been infected with the more virulent form as well, to test the vaccine. If Sri wanted to be absolutely sure she would not succumb, she would have done exactly that. Egill meant nothing to Sri. What was one slave to her? Ghost burned with fury to think anyone who had taken a witch's vows could cause such harm.

To work off the anger, Ghost threw himself into cleaning. He found plenty to be washed, and he opened windows to air out the rooms. The hearth in the main room was burning well, and he added a log to make sure the bedroom was warm. He was not about to let Gerry catch a chill, not when Gerry was so weak. Ghost brought in more wood from the yard and went back out to feed the chickens and gather eggs.

Those chores done, Ghost found fresh sheets and comfortable clothing for Gerry and took them into the bedroom. Gerry still looked far too pale for Ghost's comfort, but Ghost wanted to believe that he felt cooler. Egill was still sitting on the very edge of the bed, and he offered Ghost a reassuring smile.

"You need to eat," Ghost told Egill. "I'm going to make you something, and we can clean up in here after you've finished, all right?"

Egill nodded and waved for Ghost to go back out to the main room. The boy's attention was on Gerry, and Ghost felt a rush of gratitude for Egill's help.

Ghost forced himself to concentrate on preparing tea and food. He could not bear to see Gerry like this. He could not even begin to fathom the possibility of losing the man he loved so deeply. The very thought was enough to make his heart race and his throat tighten with grief.

Ghost, he's waking, I think. Egill's cry was urgent. Ghost dropped the cups he was holding and rushed to the bedroom.

Gerry's eyes fluttered, and he stirred beneath the quilt. Egill stood and moved aside to let Ghost get close. Ghost reached out to cup Gerry's cheek.

"Gerry? I'm home, love. I'm here. Open your eyes," Ghost said. Gerry felt cooler, and Ghost was dizzy with relief when he realized the fever had broken. "Moon shine on me, I missed you, love."

Gerry's eyes opened, unfocused at first. Ghost broke into a smile when he saw the familiar green and brown mix, and his own lashes grew damp. He stroked Gerry's stubbled cheek with tender fingers.

"Ghost?" Gerry's voice was raspy, and he coughed. "Dry."

I'll bring water. Gerry's eyes followed Egill as he slipped out of the room.

"Don't try to talk, love. You were infected. You were burning up with fever when I got here." Ghost's fingers continued to explore Gerry's cheek almost of their own volition. "We have the cure, and you're going to be fine, love."

Ghost helped Gerry to sit up and adjusted the pillows to support him. Egill returned, and Ghost took the cup and held it to Gerry's lips. Gerry's eyes darted to Egill as he sipped, and Egill watched Gerry with equal curiosity.

Ghost took the cup away when it was still half full and set it to one side. "Enough for now. Too much and we'll set your stomach off again. I think you've purged enough."

Gerry leaned back against the pile of pillows. "S'better," he said, though his voice was still rough. "You found the Witch?"

"Yes," Ghost said. "Or maybe she found me. I'm not quite sure. But we can talk when you're feeling stronger. I'm just so glad your fever is gone and you woke up. You need to rest a little more, all right? I'll be here. I'm not leaving, love." Gerry closed his eyes, still pale, but Ghost could see the color returning to his cheeks.

Relief made Ghost giddy, and he stroked Gerry's forehead with a gentle hand. Egill waited quietly until Ghost turned around, brushing away the tears from his cheeks. "He's sleeping again. I said I'd feed you, right?"

AFTER FEEDING THE boy, Ghost let Egill sit with Gerry while he went out to wash the contents of the basket in the washhouse. The chore occupied his hands and helped the time to pass, and Egill proved to be an attentive assistant.

Gerry dozed for a short time before he woke again, and Egill summoned Ghost at once. Ghost hurried into the bedroom, his heart lighter when he saw Gerry's weak smile.

"You look better, love. The antidote's working," Ghost said, sitting next to Gerry. "The fever's gone, and you have a little more color. You scared me half to death, you know. I thought I'd lost you."

"Not that easy to get rid of me," Gerry whispered. He licked dry lips, and Ghost reached for the cup of water to offer him a drink. "You did it?"

"I found the Witch. She found Egill after Tal smuggled him out of the West Reaches, and Egill was the one who actually found the cure. It's a crazy story, love."

"Still want to hear it." Gerry's voice was stronger, and he gave Egill an appraising look. To Ghost's delight, Egill did not shrink back.

Ghost beckoned Egill closer. "Egill was taken by the slavers and sold to a witch in the West Reaches. She despised the idea of a male witch enough to create a deadly virus. The idea was to make me look incapable, and this Wester witch, Sri, would have swooped in to the rescue. But in the meantime, how many have died? Four hands, or is it five now?"

Gerry frowned. "At least three hands, maybe more." The words seemed to tire him, and he peered at Ghost. "I'm sorry. After you left, I saw Natali do the same thing. I was wrong."

"Hush. Everything's all right. I should have worked harder to make you see and not merely take offense, like I did." Ghost shook his head. "We both have to learn in our own way. So, where was I?" He caressed Gerry's cheek with gentle fingers. "Sri and her accomplice also created the cure, or more precisely, the antidote to the sickness and a vaccine to make a person immune to it. One component of the antidote can only be found in the Northlands. They thought the difficulty in collecting all the ingredients would keep anyone from figuring out the cure on their own, and they were probably right. But they forgot one thing."

Gerry looked interested, and Ghost was pleased. He knew he was not a natural storyteller, but Gerry always seemed to like to listen to him, and so he continued. "The Northers are all taught to read and write. They keep the books they find, Gerry, stacks and stacks of books. I was so amazed." He lowered his voice. "I got some books to keep. The godsmen will have fits if they find out, but I couldn't say no. I'll call the books witch records if they find them."

Gerry managed a small chuckle that ended in a cough, and Ghost offered him more water. Gerry waved the cup off when he had taken several sips, and Ghost picked up the thread of his story.

"But anyway, Egill knew how to read, and he read Sri's notes. Not only did he read them, he remembered them exactly, and wrote them out for the Witch. Tal, one of the witchsisters, rescued him from Sri and smuggled Egill onto a carriage headed to the Northlands. Egill brought some of the antidote and vaccine with him, supplies Sri and her accomplice had prepared in advance. The Witch intercepted the carriage and went north with Egill, and that's where I met them. So Egill's the one who's saved us." Ghost reached out to tug a flustered and shy Egill closer. "He didn't want to stay in the Northlands, so he came with us."

Gerry looked at Ghost with a faint smile, his color nearly back to normal. Ghost returned the smile, relief brightening it. "But enough of my chatter. What happened, love? Aside from the obvious, since I know you got sick. How did it start?"

"I had a headache," Gerry said, and his brow furrowed as he thought back. "I was helping at the infirmary, and when I left, I had a headache. I didn't want to ask Natali for help, so I went home instead." He paused for a few more sips of water. "I went to wash before I came into the house. My headache got worse, and my stomach started. It all went fast from there. I remember getting sick a few times, and I hurt all over. For the most part, I stayed in bed. I thought I heard you once or twice, but I think I was dreaming. Or maybe it was wishful thinking."

"I'm here now." Ghost turned to Egill. "I'll bring Gerry some broth, and I can help him wash up and change. Afterward, I could use your help to change the sheets."

GERRY MANAGED A bowl of broth and two slices of fresh bread before he declared himself both full and exhausted. He let Ghost wash him with a soft cloth and warm water, not quite as thorough as a scrubbing in the washhouse, but enough to clean away most of the dried sweat and blood. Gerry was stubborn enough to insist on dressing himself. Ghost watched him, wary, while Egill helped change the sheets.

Egill spent the night at Gerry and Ghost's house. Ghost tucked him into bed in the back bedroom, not wanting to send Egill back through the strange streets to the infirmary. The boy seemed happy enough to stay, and Ghost had one fewer worry for the night.

After settling Egill in, Ghost went into his own bedroom and closed the door. He stripped in haste and thought about finding one of his knitted tunics, but Gerry's voice stopped him.

"I've missed seeing you like this, all pale and silvery in the moonlight." Gerry was watching Ghost with undisguised appreciation, and Ghost put his hands on his hips.

"You've been feverish and sick for at least two days. You need to rest, not get yourself all worked up," Ghost scolded, but he smiled anyway. The truth was he enjoyed seeing the admiration in Gerry's eyes, a look reserved just for him.

"You've cured me," Gerry said, a hint of laughter in his voice. "I'm feeling much better, beloved. Come to bed?"

A fluttering in Ghost's belly matched a growing interest elsewhere. "To sleep," he said, doing his best to sound stern despite his treacherous body.

"Of course to sleep," Gerry agreed, and he folded back the quilt in invitation.

Ghost climbed into the bed and slipped into Gerry's warm embrace. "Oh, love, I've missed you," he admitted. Ghost settled into Gerry's arms, his head on Gerry's shoulder. Ghost wrapped an arm around Gerry's broad chest. "Pillows don't really do the trick."

"I noticed," Gerry said, and he turned his head to press a kiss to the top of Ghost's head. "I missed you too, beloved. This place was empty without you. And I'm not sure I'm going to be able to fall asleep, now I have you next to me again."

"Oh, don't you dare, or I'll go make hemp again," Ghost said, lifting his head to look at Gerry. "You need to sleep to heal properly. We can wait until the morning and see how you are then."

"Mm." Gerry shifted, and his thigh pressed against Ghost's hard cock. "I can see what you mean. Or feel it, actually."

A shiver ran through Ghost as Gerry moved again, creating a delicious friction against Ghost's cock. "Ignore it. It's just what a man's body will do," he said, unconsciously echoing Njall's words.

"Yes, it is." Gerry's voice held a husky note that promised he was not about to let this slide. "A man's body will do many things, especially when he's got the man he loves in his arms. In case you hadn't noticed, I'm interested too, my precious Ghost. I don't want to wait until morning."

"You've been sick," Ghost protested, but it was a feeble effort. He raised himself on one elbow and looked at Gerry, trying to ignore the tent in the quilt.

"Moon shine on me, Ghost. When you look at me like this, how can I even think about anything but making love to you?" Gerry's smile took Ghost's breath away. "I'll let you do all the work, beloved. I promise. But please let me feel you. Father help me, I thought I'd ruined everything. I was so scared you wouldn't come home to me."

"I couldn't leave you," Ghost said. "I see things differently because I'm a witch, or maybe because I grew up with no one other than the Witch for company. I don't always get how life works, and I know it. I also know I don't want to be anywhere you're not." Ghost moved, rising up onto his knees.

Gerry lifted his hips, and Ghost pulled down the woven pants Ghost had given him to wear. His cock was standing strong and erect and already beaded with precome. Ghost took in the sight of Gerry's naked body and shifted to straddle him.

"This is good, beloved." Gerry wrapped callused hands around Ghost's hips. "I'll let you take what you want, my precious Ghost."

"I want you," Ghost said, and he leaned forward to kiss Gerry, relishing the scrape of stubble against his lips and chin. Gerry's fingers slid into his hair as Gerry pulled him into the kiss. Gerry's cock pressed against Ghost's thigh, and Ghost abandoned Gerry's lips in favor of kissing his way down Gerry's neck. Gerry's pulse beat strong against Ghost's lips, encouraging Ghost to move his attentions a good bit lower.

Ghost breathed in, the scent of Gerry's precome as intoxicating as it was familiar. He licked his lips before lowering his mouth over the head of Gerry's cock, hearing the delighted gasp that escaped Gerry. He let the tip of his tongue tease the sensitive cleft under the head until he had coaxed a needy moan from Gerry. Ghost savored Gerry's taste, his mouth sliding down the shaft nearly half the way.

Gerry's fingers tightened in Ghost's hair, and Ghost could see the way Gerry's belly tensed. Ghost slipped one hand under Gerry's balls, cupping them. He stroked the tender patch behind the sac, and Gerry moaned again, a sound that ran straight to Ghost's belly in a rush of heat. He drew his lips up with deliberate slowness and sank back down again, taking almost all of Gerry's cock. His tongue traced the thick vein along the underside of the shaft as he drew his mouth off Gerry's cock, sucking as he went.

"Ghost," Gerry whispered, and his voice was husky with need. Ghost glanced up, loving this flush in Gerry's cheeks, and the heat in his eyes. Gerry tugged to pull Ghost up into a kiss. Ghost fumbled for the oil in the little basket, nipping Gerry's lower lip as Gerry deepened the kiss.

Ghost let his body say all the things he had no words for. His sorrow over their argument. His regret at having to leave with the disagreement unresolved. His fear upon seeing Gerry so ill. He could not get enough of Gerry. He opened into the kiss as Gerry plumbed his mouth. He could feel his nipples tighten as they brushed against Gerry's chest, the peaks sensitive to the lightest touch. Gerry's hand closed over Ghost's and took the oil from him. Ghost gasped in pure need as Gerry's hand caressed the curve of his buttocks.

"My precious Ghost," Gerry murmured, his breath hot against Ghost's ear. "I've missed you. I've missed this."

Gerry's finger, slippery with oil, traced the entrance between Ghost's cheeks. He pressed back, wanting to be breached. He needed to be filled, to know he and Gerry were whole again. Ghost's world dwindled down to this moment, one bow-roughened finger buried inside him. Ghost heard his own soft gasp at the welcome intrusion. Ghost's cock jumped, leaving a wet mark on Gerry's belly.

"How's this, beloved?" Gerry's whisper sent a tingle down Ghost's spine, and Ghost pressed back against Gerry's hand, demanding and needy. "I'll take this as approval, shall I? Or do you want more?"

"You talk too much," Ghost informed him, and his cock twitched as Gerry added a second finger. Ghost's hole loosened at Gerry's familiar touch. At the same time, the touch heightened his desire. Ghost's restless fingers worked their way into Gerry's thick hair, tugging him into another kiss, because Gerry's mouth was made to be kissed.

When they broke apart, Ghost gazed down at Gerry, drinking in the expression on his face. "Now," he whispered. "I'm ready. I need you."

"Are you sure?" The question was their ritual. Gerry was already grasping Ghost's hips, helping Ghost line up his hole with Gerry's oil-slicked cock. Ghost pressed down, impatient to be filled, his hands gripping Gerry's forearms for leverage.

Ghost watched Gerry's eyes flutter closed as Ghost's passage accepted the head of Gerry's cock. Ghost eased himself down on Gerry's cock until Gerry's balls brushed against Ghost's cheeks. Gerry was inside him as far as it was possible. Ghost was home.

Strong hands held Ghost in place, and Ghost wriggled against the restraint, his back bowing as Gerry's cock ground within him. The movement hit all the right places and sent sparks of pleasure up Ghost's spine.

"Give it a moment," Gerry said. "Let yourself adjust."

"I need to move." The words came out as a growl, and Gerry chuckled as Ghost wriggled again.

"Fierce little thing." Gerry loosened his grip, though.

Ghost rolled his hips forward to ride Gerry's cock, his thighs flexing as he lifted himself. His hands tightened around Gerry's forearms. Ghost gasped, sliding back down as Gerry's cock found the sweet spot inside him. At the same time, Gerry's hand wrapped around Ghost's cock, squeezing tight. The room disappeared in a flash of white behind Ghost's eyes.

All the need, and desire, and worry found release in the cry Ghost could not hold back. He was aware, somewhere in the back of his mind, how his balls had tightened. He could feel the throb of the thick vein along the underside of Gerry's cock as his passage closed around it. He ground down, wanting all of Gerry. His hips rocked again, and Ghost gasped as a glorious wave of sensation burst through him. He rode Gerry with frantic and erratic thrusts as he spasmed around Gerry's cock. His balls pulsed, and his come emptied onto Gerry's taut stomach.

"Ghost," Gerry whispered, rough and ragged. "Oh, beloved, Moon shine on me, you feel so good. I can't wait." The heat of Gerry's release filled Ghost and sent a whole new burst of pleasure spiraling upward along his spine to explode behind his eyes.

Ghost let himself fall forward, trusting Gerry to catch him. His heart was beating like a drum, and he buried his face in the warm space between Gerry's shoulder and neck, breathing in the familiar scent of Gerry's skin. Gerry's rough fingers rubbed along Ghost's back. Ghost trembled as he wrapped his arms around Gerry as best he could. The journey was over.

"Next time, you're coming with me," Ghost mumbled into Gerry's neck, listening to the comfortable thrum of Gerry's pulse.

"Next time?" Gerry sounded amused, and Ghost lifted his head to peer at Gerry. "Only if I get to pick where we go. The Northlands? Way too cold for me, even with a hot-blooded mate like mine." Gerry's lips muffled Ghost's laughing protest. Ghost settled in his arms. They exchanged soft kisses for a while until Ghost's head fell back against the pillows. Gerry's hum of contentment filled his ears and heart as he drifted off to sleep.

Epilogue

AS THE SUN rose the next morning, Ghost dressed to visit the infirmary and check on the effectiveness of the cure. If Gerry was any indication, the antidote worked exactly as Sri's notes promised. Egill was already dressed and waiting to go too. Ghost agreed he could come along, but first Ghost returned to the bedroom to say goodbye to Gerry.

"I'm going with you," Gerry insisted.

"You're still recovering," Ghost argued. But Gerry was already out of bed and pulling on his breeches. Ghost did not fight further because, in truth, he was reluctant to leave Gerry, even for a morning.

All the surviving afflicted were recovering well, and Ghost gave anyone who had not had the illness a prophylactic dose of the vaccine. The Witch and Natali assisted in the vaccinations, and Natali thanked Ghost again for the gifts he had given her. She left to return to her own village, promising to contact Ghost for updates on the epidemic and the cure. For her part, the Witch went back to her house outside town to start the proceedings against Sri and Tarah.

Gerry, Ghost, and Egill returned home at the end of the day, and Ghost prepared a hearty meal for Gerry to help him regain his strength. After dinner, Egill settled in to read in the back bedroom as Ghost cleaned up the dinner dishes. Ghost felt Gerry's presence at his back, and he turned from the sink to see Gerry standing in the doorway. Gerry's cheeks were a hectic pink.

"Is everything all—"

"I... This is hard." Gerry interrupted Ghost's question. "When you were gone... Sometimes it's difficult to tell you how I feel."

Ghost nodded, clutching a cup in his hands. Gerry sat by the hearth and lowered his eyes, looking at his fingers as they twined together in his lap.

"I'm sorry I haven't been as good a mate to you as you deserve. I promised to respect your decisions as a healer, and the first time that was put to the test, I failed you. I thought I was doing the right thing by letting you go when you told me you had to leave, but the truth is I failed you again." Gerry paused, looking for words, and Ghost could only watch. "I need you to forgive me. I need to know we're all right, because I can't imagine my life without you at my side. I don't ever want you to leave again, but if you have to go, don't leave me behind, beloved. I can't bear it. You're all I'll ever need, and wherever you are is home."

Ghost felt his lashes grow damp. He dropped the cup and launched himself into Gerry's arms. "Oh, Gerry, I'm back. I won't leave again. You're my home, love." Ghost blinked away hot tears. "You're all I need too. I promise I'll never leave you. I'll stay right here in your arms where I belong. I love you. Moon shine on me, Gerry. I love you."

Ghost swallowed the rest of what he wanted to say in a sob. He gripped Gerry's tunic tightly, fisting his hands in the fabric and breathing in the scent of his mate. Ghost felt a fool for crying, but Gerry stood strong and rubbed Ghost's back in a soothing rhythm until Ghost's sobs eased.

"I was wondering," Gerry murmured into Ghost's ear. "The Witch is making noises about going to the South for the hearing, isn't she?"

Ghost drew a shaky breath and leaned back into Gerry's embrace, puzzled by the change in topic. "So I've gathered. I'm pretty sure Zereda is presiding, so it'll be in the South. All the elder witches will hear the case."

"What's she going to do with Egill? Is she taking him too?" Gerry pressed a kiss to Ghost's hair.

"I don't know. I suppose it's his choice. Isn't it? He's got no family we know of, and the clan I met isn't his." Ghost gazed into Gerry's eyes, trying to *see* what he was thinking.

"How would you feel about taking Egill as our dependent?" Gerry's smile was mischievous.

Ghost gasped. He was planning on asking Gerry the same thing this evening when they were alone. Ghost wanted Egill more than anything. Ghost knew how lost and alone Egill must feel right now. Ghost had felt the same way living with the Witch. An outcast because he looked different, because he could *see*. No matter how hard the Witch tried, he never felt as though he belonged until Gerry came along and loved him. Egill would have what Ghost never had. Egill would have Ghost, who looked like Egill, and *saw* like Egill. And Egill would have Gerry, to cherish Egill with a father's devotion and not question what Egill was.

"Why are you asking me?" Ghost demanded. "I mean, you're the alpha, you know." Ghost placed his palms flat against Gerry's chest.

"Well, yes, but I'd rather have the advice of my wise and fierce witch before I make such a momentous decision."

Gerry laughed as Ghost twined his hands in Gerry's hair and pulled him down into a heated kiss.

When Ghost finally let him up for air, Gerry gazed into Ghost's eyes and smiled. "I'll take the kiss for a yes." Ghost opened his mouth to speak, but Gerry touched his finger to

Ghost's lips to stop him. "And I'm also going to tell you I'm the happiest man in the village right now. I love you, Ghost. I can't imagine a life without you by my side. But more important, I can't imagine not being at your side. You're all I need to make my life complete, and wherever life takes us, we'll go together. Even if it means going to your frozen Northlands."

"Just as long as we're together," Ghost said, looking into Gerry's eyes and seeing only love there. "We can take the carriage up to the Northlands in the summer. You, and me, and our Egill. Our family."

About the Author

Morwen has been writing since she could first hold a pencil, and by all accounts she didn't limit herself to paper. Walls, tablecloths and the occasional sibling were all fair game, and it shouldn't be surprising to learn that markers were banned in her home with all due haste. Although she now contents herself with inconveniencing electrons, the desire to bring the stories in her mind to life hasn't waned.

In her spare time, she reads, putters in the kitchen, and relaxes on her terrace or at the lake, weather permitting, with her corgi who strives to be part muse, part food disposal. She's also addicted to coffee and has a close relationship with her Keurig.

Email: morwennavarre@gmail.com

Facebook: www.facebook.com/morwen.navarre

Twitter: @BronxWench

Website: www.bronxwench.blogspot.com

Other books by this author

Ghost's Sight

Also Available from NineStar Press

Connect with NineStar Press

Website: NineStarPress.com

Facebook: NineStarPress

Facebook Reader Group: NineStarNiche

Twitter: @ninestarpress

Tumblr: NineStarPress